D0011318

SLIDER

SLIDER

PETE HAUTMAN

CANDLEWICK PRESS

Copyright © 2017 by Pete Hautman

First paperback edition 2018

Library of Congress Catalog Card Number 2017953738
ISBN 978-0-7636-9070-0 (hardcover)
ISBN 978-1-5362-0432-2 (paperback)

22 23 24 TRC 10 9 8 7 6

Printed in Eagan, MN, U.S.A.

This book was typeset in Melior.

Candlewick Press
99 Dover Street
Somerville, Massachusetts 02144

visit us at www.candlewick.com

For Nancy and Steve

⟨ 1 ⟩

PIZZA

A sixteen-inch pizza, fresh from the oven, is a thing of beauty.

Disks of pepperoni shimmer and glisten on a sea of molten mozzarella. Dark-red oregano-flecked sauce bubbles up through the cheese, surrounded by a hand-tossed, artfully charred crust.

"Well?" HeyMan says. It's only two in the afternoon, and a five-o'clock shadow is already winning the battle for his face. Hayden Mankowski—that's his real name—is the hairiest kid I know. He's been shaving since he was ten.

I push my finger into the middle of the pizza. "Still too hot." I lick my finger.

"You started," he says.

"That doesn't count."

HeyMan looks at Cyn, who is folded into the booth across from us.

"Cyn? Does the finger-lick count?"

Cyn's wrists are resting atop her knees, and she's holding her phone about three inches from her nose. Her straight black hair hangs over her forehead and into her eyes. She looks like a smartphone with bangs. Her thumbs move, and her phone makes a faint *whoosh*. Cyn is obsessed with her new phone. She says she's going the whole day communicating via text messages only. *Verbal communication is so last millennium*, she texted me this morning.

Cyn, HeyMan, and I are the Three Musketeers, even though we have no muskets, and Cyn is the only one who has actually read the book. We have been best friends since before HeyMan started shaving. Next fall we will all be starting high school together.

HeyMan checks his cell for her text.

"She says it doesn't count," he says after a moment. He lifts a slice of his sausage-and-mushroom. "Mine's not that hot," he says, taking a bite from the tip. I notice he follows it quickly with a gulp of Dew.

I shake my head and wait patiently for that magic moment when the sauce is not deadly hot but the cheese is still soft. A minute later, HeyMan takes another, more cautious bite.

"Seriously," he says, swallowing. "It's not."

"Okay," I say. "Time me."

HeyMan puts down his slice and, with a greasy fore finger, pulls up the stopwatch function on his phone and touches the start button. "Go!"

I go.

It is not the best pizza ever. The cheese has turned rubbery and the crust in the middle is kind of gooey. I down the whole thing in four minutes and thirty-six seconds.

HeyMan groans, pulls out his wallet, and hands me a ten-dollar bill.

I grab the tenner with one hand and a slice of HeyMan's sausage-and-mushroom pizza with the other, because I'm still kind of hungry.

"You're a freak." HeyMan puts away his wallet. "I don't get how come you're not, like, huge."

"I have this metabolism," I say.

"Yeah, a really freaky metabolism," HeyMan says. "I bet you got a tapeworm a mile long."

I laugh. My phone chirps.

I look at Cyn. Unfolded, she is as tall as me—five seven and a quarter—but folded, she is quite small. She is like one of those pop-up campers.

I check my phone.

> **37 ft.**

"What?" I say.

I hardly see her thumbs move. Cyn Lee's texting skills are superhuman.

My phone chirps.

> **Tapeworms**

I make a disgusted face. Cyn does not look directly at me, but her lips curve into a smile.

"What's she saying?" HeyMan asks.

"She's riffing on your tapeworm theme," I say.

Cyn's thumbs dance. I look at my phone, waiting with dread and curiosity for the text to arrive.

> **120 feet in whales.**

"Did you just look that up, or is it something you already knew?" I ask.

She just smiles. Of course she already knew. Cyn is a trivia monster.

"How long do they get in dogs?" I ask.

I asked about dogs because I have to give Arfie these chewy things every month just in case he has worms which he probably does because he eats rabbit turds in the backyard. Arfie is actually Mal's dog, but I'm the one who has to take care of him. Mal can't be trusted with taking-care-of-dog stuff.

More about Mal later.

I saw this guy on TV who eats all kinds of weird things like maggots and ostrich guts. I could never do that. In fact, I have a rather sophisticated palate. I like lobster and artichokes and stuff like that. When I'm hungry I can eat just about anything, but I draw the line at maggots. There are many things I will not eat. Sauerkraut and pickled pigs' feet, for example. Or if HeyMan wanted to bet me ten dollars that I couldn't eat a bunch of rabbit turds, he could keep his money.

Arfie, he'd take that bet in a heartbeat.

HeyMan and I are done eating, but Cyn is just getting started on her kid-size Veggie Deluxe. I think she must be making a point, because I've seen her eat a lot faster. She picks a mushroom from her pizza and eats it slowly, showing me how it's done.

"You're supposed to eat the whole thing, not pick it apart and take like an hour a slice," I tell her. "The whole *point* of a pizza is that everything is all together."

Cyn pretends to ignore me and takes the smallest possible nibble from her scrap of mushroom, just to bug me. She still has three-quarters of her pizza to go.

"Sonya Thomas would've downed that whole thing in about thirty seconds," I say. Sonya Thomas, aka the Black Widow, is this 105-pound Korean-American woman who once ate five hundred and sixty-four oysters in eight minutes for the world record.

Cyn glares at me, her eyes narrowing. "I am *not* Sonya Thomas," she says, verbally.

"You talked!" I say.

She glares harder.

"And I didn't mean 'cause she's Korean," I say. "I meant 'cause she's a girl."

"You are an idiot." She plucks a sliver of onion from her miniature pie and places it delicately on her tongue.

While we wait for Cyn to finish her pizza, HeyMan and I talk about a python-eating-a-goat video we saw on YouTube. Cyn is playing with her phone, ignoring us and taking a small bite every so often.

"A whole goat—that would be like eating twenty pizzas at once," HeyMan says.

"Joey Chestnut could do it." Joey Chestnut is the most famous eater in the world. He once ate seventy hot dogs in ten minutes.

"I thought you were a Jooky fan."

"I am. Joey had the advantage that day. He's like two hundred thirty pounds. Jooky's only one fifty, and he only got beat by half a dog."

I saw it on YouTube. Jooky Garafalo downed sixty-nine and a half hot dogs in ten minutes. But what was weird was he was trying to beat Joey, and ho couldn't get that last half dog down. I mean, I couldn't imagine not being able to eat half a hot dog no matter how full I was, especially if it was for the world record. But I guess that just makes it even more amazing because you just know that Jooky had to have taken it right to the absolute limit if he had to stop at sixty-nine and a half.

"Jooky's got heart," I say.

HeyMan's phone chirps. I know it's Cyn, because she's got that little smile. HeyMan checks the message, smiles confusedly, and shows it to me.

> "The merit of all things lies in their difficulty."

"Shakespeare?" I guess.

The Three Musketeers, Cyn says. Verbally.

BACON AND OLIVES

My name is the incredibly ordinary and common and boring David Alan Miller. No one knows how many other David Millers there are, but it's got to be roughly equal to the population of Wyoming. I have never been to Wyoming the state, but I have been to Wyoming, Minnesota, and there are definitely enough David Millers to fill up that little town. When I turn eighteen, the first thing I'm going to do is change my name. I'll still be David Miller, but it'll be something like David *Fuzzbucket* Miller. I'll call myself Fuzz. Or maybe Fuzzy. Alan was my grandfather's name. He died when I was two. He owned a bar in Solon Springs, Wisconsin, but he sold it when he retired back in the eighties, which gives you some idea how old he was. My mom grew up in Solon Springs. She says she is never going back. She also says I got my metabolism from my dad's side of the family. My dad is hyper. He is constantly doing stuff like crosscutting the grass or painting the house or patching the driveway. Dad likes things neat.

It gets really cold here in Vacaville, Iowa, and every winter we get these big cracks in the driveway. My dad is all about patching driveway cracks. You would think it was his skin that was cracking. So our driveway is covered with these black squiggles and the stuff gets soft in the summer so it's no good trying to skateboard on it because the wheels stick in the patches and you could kill yourself in like one second. And it gets on Arfie's paws, which he hates and tries to bite off.

Arfie will eat anything. Tar and rabbit turds are the least of it.

When I get home my mom is making—guess what—pizza! Not kidding. She buys these premade pizza crusts and slathers all kinds of stuff on top and pops it in the oven and calls it pizza. One time she used catsup instead of regular pizza sauce and I could tell right away, but this time she's using canned pizza sauce, with Canadian bacon and green olives, which sounds gross but she's made it before and it's pretty good if you like salty pizza.

"I just ate an entire pepperoni pizza," I say.

She looks at me and does this exaggerated shoulder

sag, as if I'd dissed a dinner she'd been working on for hours. But I didn't mean it that way; I was just saying it was like a coincidence.

"I didn't say I wasn't hungry," I add.

That produces an eye roll, one notch above a shoulder sag.

"Where do you put it?" she asks.

That is what my dad calls a *rhetorical* question. I answer her anyway.

"I think I have cow stomachs," I say. "Like, two stomachs?"

"That would explain so much." My mother has what you call a dry sense of humor. A lot of the time I don't even know when she is trying to be funny. "Your father called. He won't be home for another couple of hours."

When my dad is not patching the driveway or poisoning dandelions or caulking invisible cracks around the windows or trimming the bushes to within a millimeter of each other he sells commercial refrigeration units. It's not very interesting so I won't go into it. But he's always driving back and forth to Des Moines, about an hour away from Vacaville.

I hear a car pull up. I look out the window. Bridgette and Derek. Bridgette is my older sister. She's in college, but her school is only half an hour away, so she comes home for dinner once a week or so. She says it's to make

Mom happy. Derek is her idiot boyfriend. Both of them are so crazy for college that they take classes in the middle of summer, and both of them have jobs on campus—Bridgette works in the admissions office, and Derek is the caretaker for his fraternity house.

"The droids are here," I say. I call them that because Derek reminds me of C-3PO from *Star Wars* if you can imagine Threepio with a ponytail, glasses, and skin. Fortunately, Bridgette doesn't look like R2-D2, but she's just as smart.

Mom slides the first pizza into the oven.

"Mal is in his room," she says. I hadn't asked about Mal, but Mom is big on pop-up news flashes. "Why don't you check on him?"

Checking on Mal is a never-ending task. We are all about checking on Mal. We've been checking on him since he was born, and that was ten years ago.

‹ 3 ›

Potato Chips

Mal's door is closed. I give it the special knock he likes—*bip, bippity-bip-bip . . . bip-bip*—and walk in. Mal is sitting cross-legged on his bed, rocking back and forth, staring happily at his Wall of Things. Mal is all about his Things. The wall at the end of his bed is covered with them. It is an impressive collection. If you like Things.

"Hey Mal," I say.

Arfie, a brown furry puddle on the floor next to the bed, raises his shaggy head and looks up at me. Mal just keeps on rocking and staring at his Wall. Mal loves to rock. Mom calls it his "exercises." He's been doing it since he was a baby.

"Nice to see you, too," I say.

I check his Wall to see if he's added any new Things. It's hard to tell. The Wall is so covered with Things there's hardly any wall left to see.

"Is that a new feather?" I ask.

Mal nods, or maybe he's just rocking more vigorously.

I was just guessing about the feather. There are so many feathers thumbtacked to his Wall there's no way I could pick out a new one.

Most of Mal's Things come from our fenced-in backyard, where he and Arfie hang out when the weather is nice. Dad keeps our yard immaculate, but Mal manages to find something almost every day. The rules are that every Thing has to be Mom-approved, and only then is he allowed to attach it to his Wall.

Things Mom will allow:
Leaves
Butterfly wings
Feathers
Flower petals

Things Mom will not allow:
Whole insects, living or dead
Rabbit turds
Worms

Mal is very good about following rules, once he accepts them. When he first started decorating his Wall he brought in everything from live slugs to used paper napkins. There were a few meltdowns. We had a talk about it, me and Mal and Bridgette and Mom and Dad — a family meeting, which as usual was mostly Mom and Dad talking, me half listening, Bridgette examining her fingernails, and Mal off in his own world, flapping his hands and avoiding our eyes. But Mom knows how to lay down the law with Mal, and after a while he got with the leaf/feather/flower/butterfly-wing program. Still, every so often he tries to sneak in some squirrel hair or a dead grasshopper.

"Time to eat, Mal," I say. "Pizza."

Mal stops rocking and tilts his head, listening. We can hear Bridgette and Derek talking downstairs. Mal frowns.

"No pizza for you?" I ask.

The rocking resumes.

"Okay," I say, and I leave him to his exercises.

By the time I get back to the kitchen, Mom is putting the first pizza on the table.

"Mal isn't hungry," I say, but nobody looks at me. Bridgette is bragging about how she got a perfect score on some test. Bridgette is always getting perfect scores on tests. When she stops to take a breath, Derek informs my mother that in Italy, pizzas are made with water-buffalo mozzarella.

"Well, this is *Kraft* mozzarella," my mother says.

"It's all good," Derek says, trying to be polite, but coming off like a know-it-all, as usual.

I mentioned earlier that Derek is an idiot. I don't mean he is unintelligent. He gets straight A's like Bridgette and he knows a lot of stuff, but he is too stupid to realize that nobody cares that *pi* has been calculated to umpteen digits or that fourteen American presidents have been left-handed or that Italians eat cheese made out of water-buffalo milk.

I grab a slice of pizza and say, "Four minutes and thirty-six seconds."

Everybody looks at me.

"That's how fast I ate a sixteen-inch pepperoni pizza today."

Bridgette rolls her eyes, exactly like mom's eye roll. Mom sighs and sags.

Derek is the only one who seems impressed. He says, "Seriously?"

"Yup. I won ten bucks."

Derek thinks for a moment, then says, "Who paid for the pizza?"

"I did."

"So you didn't actually turn a profit." Derek majors in business.

I shrug. "I got to eat the pizza."

"Four minutes and . . . how many seconds?"

"Thirty-six."

Derek takes a bite and chews thoughtfully.

"That's pretty fast," he says. "How fast can you eat that slice?"

I shove the slice in my mouth. One bite, two bites, three bites . . . and it's gone.

Bridgette and my mom are staring at me with identical horrified expressions.

Bridgette says, "Wow, that's disgusting even for you."

Derek says, "Cool!"

My mom says, "David, if you're going to eat like that, I'll just feed you and Arfie out of the same bowl."

"Sorry," I say, but I'm not.

Mom closes her eyes and takes a deep breath. "Please let Mal know it's time to come to the table."

"I already did. He isn't hungry."

"Try again." By which she means, *Please leave for a moment so I don't have to deal with you.*

Mal is still not interested in coming to the table. He has acquired a large bag of potato chips and is happily sitting on his bed and chowing down, crumbs everywhere, with Arfie sitting at the foot of the bed, begging. Mal and Arfie have bonded over potato chips. It is one of the things Mal

< 16 >

eats. The other things Mal eats are crisp-fried fish sticks, Ritz crackers, Cheerios, and pizza crust. Normally he would come down for pizza crust, but not when he has potato chips. Also, Mal does not care for Derek, who always talks to him in an extra-loud voice and smiles too much.

Mal is an excellent judge of character.

"Mal has potato chips," I say when I return to the kitchen.

Mom does her eye roll, sigh, and sag—all in one take.

"How does he do that? I hid them in the dryer."

"Mal always finds them," Bridgette says. "He must be clairvoyant."

"Clairvoyance is a myth," Derek says.

"I wasn't serious," Bridgette says.

"How was I supposed to know that?" Derek says.

"Sorry. I guess I should have added a smiley face."

Derek nods, agreeing with her. As if she was serious.

"Maybe he has super senses," I say. "He can sniff out potato chips like a bloodhound."

Derek nods and makes his thoughtful face. "Enhanced sensory capability has been observed in autistics."

"We don't call Mal the *A*-word," I say.

Derek looks confused.

"We don't like to use labels," Mom says.

"We label him Mal," I say.

⟨ 4 ⟩

PULVERIZED COW

I try to avoid using labels in front of Mom. But I use them all the time when she's not around. I label Derek an idiot, I label Bridgette an overachieving priss-butt, I label Arfie a dog, and I label myself the beef in a SooperSlider. You know what a SooperSlider is, right? It's like a White Castle. We don't have White Castles in Iowa, but it's the same thing: a greasy wafer of pulverized cow in a squishy bun half the size of your palm—a two- or maybe three-bite hamburger. Being the middle kid of three is like being the beef in a SooperSlider—you're just there to weld the bun together.

Most people don't think about what's inside the bun. They'd rather not know. But it's important. It's what puts the *slide* in slider.

. . .

The second pizza is Mom's veggie special—artichoke hearts, broccoli, and green pepper. I grab a slice and try to eat it slowly so as not to upset Mom. The rest of dinner is a constant stream of boasts from Bridgette punctuated by *oohs* and *ahhs* from Mom, with the occasional useless trivia erupting from Derek, and invisible me eating pizza. I'm reaching for another slice when my mom tells me to slow down.

"This is not an eating contest," she informs me. "Leave some for the rest of us."

"If you guys would eat instead of talk you wouldn't fall so far behind," I say.

Mom gets this pinched look.

"You may leave the table, David."

I grab the slice and stand up. Mom gives me a look.

"The crust is for Mal," I say.

I don't give the crust to Mal, who's full of potato chips anyway. I eat the whole thing while I wake up my computer. There are several alerts, mostly about eating contests. El Gurgitator won a chicken-wing event in Pennsylvania. Six pounds of wings in ten minutes. The results were disputed. The second-place finisher claimed that the Gurge had stuffed several wings down his shirt. Still, the Gurge won by twenty wings, and I don't see how he could have concealed that many greasy chicken wings in his shirt, but who knows? The Gurge is a controversial guy. There's even a word for getting beaten—fairly or unfairly—by El Gurgitator. They say, "You've been *Gurged*."

In other news, a Nathan's Famous qualifier is being held at the Iowa Speedway. That's in Newton, only an hour from Vacaville. If I could figure out how to get there, I'd go.

Do you know about the Nathan's contest? Since 1916, Nathan's Famous hot dogs has held a hot-dog-eating contest on the Fourth of July at Coney Island in New York. The first guy to win it, James Mullen, scarfed down thirteen hot dogs in twelve minutes. I would've kicked his butt.

In the years since, the Nathan's contestants have been managing to eat more and more dogs. In 1958, Jerry Kilcourse broke the twenty-dogs-in-ten-minutes barrier. That's thirty seconds a dog. I could eat a hot dog in thirty seconds, easy.

Slowly, over the years, as the eaters and their bellies got bigger, the record advanced. By the year 2000, a Japanese eater named Kazutoyo Arai was able to put down an impressive twenty-five and one-eighth hot dogs. That's a lot of dogs, but not beyond imagining.

Then, in 2001, things got crazy: another guy from Japan, the great Takeru Kobayashi, ate fifty.

Fifty hot dogs!

That's enough to fill a grocery bag, and he did it at a rate of fourteen seconds per dog. What was really amazing was that Kobayashi was not a big guy—he weighed only about 130 pounds at the time. The same as me.

For the next five years, Kobayashi dominated the Nathan's contest, winning every year, but in 2007 things changed again. A guy from California named Joey Chestnut blew Kobayashi away by slamming down sixty-six dogs. Now he's up to seventy.

Joey Chestnut is a phenomenal eater, no question, but I'm a Jooky Garafalo fan. A 150-pound guy who can eat sixty-nine and a half hot dogs is way more impressive than a 230-pound guy eating seventy.

Since losing to Joey Chestnut, Jooky has been lying low. But everybody expects him to turn up at the big Nathan's contest in July. I mean, how could he not?

I do a search for Jooky Garafalo and get only one recent hit. It's a link to the online auction site BuyBuy. I click on it, and I can't believe what pops up: a photo of half a hot dog sitting on a paper plate. I read the text.

INVESTMENT OF A LIFETIME!!!
Jooky Garafalo's Mortification!!!
Last year, in championship-eater
JOOKY GARAFALO's EPIC BATTLE with
JOEY CHESTNUT at NATHAN'S FAMOUS
HOT DOG EATING CONTEST,

Jooky heroically powered down 69½ dogs,
but he LOST the contest by
ONE-HALF HOT DOG.

I look back at the image. The photo must have been taken right at the end of the contest, before they cleared the plates away. It's making me hungry.

I keep reading.

This HISTORIC HALF HOT DOG has been
lovingly preserved and is now available for sale
to a discriminating collector.
MUSEUMS AND HISTORICAL SOCIETY BIDS
WELCOME!!

Last year I went to the State Historical Museum in Des Moines on a school field trip. They have a gigantic mammoth skeleton. I picture the preserved half hot dog in the same room as the mammoth. It's no contest.

The hot dog is way cooler.

I scroll down and almost fall off my chair.

Opening bid: 50¢
Number of bids: 0

Fifty *cents*? For a piece of *history*? And nobody has bid on it yet? That's *crazy*.

I imagine the half dog sitting on display on my shelf.

Below is a live ticker, counting down the hours and minutes until the close of bidding:

5 hrs. 18 min.

The auction is going to end at midnight. My heart starts pounding so hard I can hear it. I call HeyMan.

"Dude! You'll never guess what I'm looking at!"

"Prob'ly not," he says. I can tell he's eating something.

"Jooky Garafalo's hot dog!"

More chewing sounds come through the phone, and then he says, "Is that, like, a what-do-you-call-it . . . a euphemism?"

"No! It's the half hot dog Jooky couldn't eat!"

"Why are you looking at Jooky Garafalo's hot dog?"

"It's on BuyBuy! The half dog he didn't eat!"

"I don't get it." More chewing.

"It's *history*! And it's for *sale*!"

"Oh. You gonna buy it?"

I make my decision right then and there.

⟨ 5 ⟩

HALF DOG

This is my chance to own something really important. But you need a credit card or some sort of Internet money to bid on BuyBuy. I don't have anything like that.

Mom, on the other hand, has all kinds of credit cards. In fact, she once let me use her Visa to order a book I needed for school, and I wrote down the card number someplace. It takes a while, but I find it scrawled on a scrap of paper on my desk.

A few minutes later I'm registered. I bid fifty cents. My hands are shaking. I'm the high bidder. I'm the *only* bidder.

Naturally, I'll have to pay Mom back. And she'll probably be mad about me using her card without permission. But it's only fifty cents, and this is an emergency. Easier to just do it and apologize later.

I'm about to call HeyMan and tell him when my computer bings and the numbers change.

Someone else has topped my bid. The high bid is now a dollar.

I bid a dollar fifty. I watch my bid come up on the screen. Two minutes later—*bing!*—the number jumps to two dollars.

I take a deep breath. Time to pull out the big guns.

I bid three dollars and sit staring intently at the screen, willing my invisible competition to give up. This time he makes me wait a full ten minutes.

Bing! Three fifty.

I should mention here that I am very competitive when I want to be, and this other bidder is starting to bug me. I bid four dollars.

By seven thirty we're up to nine dollars, but I sense I am winning—each time I raise the bid, my opponent takes longer to come back with a higher bid. I'm getting bored. A pop-up window appears advertising an "Exciting New Feature" called AutoBuyBuy that will automatically overbid the competition until it reaches the maximum I'm willing to pay. I open my wallet. Twenty dollars in cash, and an iTunes gift card with $3.47 left on it. Pathetic.

I hear the droids drive off. A few seconds later my mother's penetrating voice snakes up the stairs and squeezes under my door and drills into my ears.

"David!"

"What!" I yell back.

"Dishes!"

"In a minute!" I shout.

"Now!"

There is no getting around it. It's my night to do dishes, and until I do them, the wheedling will not end. Quickly, I set up AutoBuyBuy for a maximum bid of twenty dollars. It's more than I planned to pay originally, but I have the money, and if I have to give my mom the last of my cash to cover her Visa bill, she'll probably be okay with that. Maybe not *exactly* okay, because I'm using her card number without permission, but she won't go ballistic. Probably.

I run downstairs and power through the cleanup routine. I don't really hate washing dishes, but there are things I'd rather be doing.

I'm wiping the countertop when Mal starts screaming.

< 26 >

‹ 6 ›

BURRITO

When Mal screams, there is nothing else in the universe but the sound of his voice. It is a black hole of sound, a shrieking vortex of fury and frustration. I drop what I'm doing and run upstairs. Mal is sitting on his bed, exactly where I left him. The only difference is that his bag of chips is empty and he's screeching. Is he screeching because his chips are gone, or because of some invisible, unknowable thing that only he can see? With Mal, there's no way to know.

I do what I always do, which is get behind him and wrap my arms around his chest and squeeze.

Sometimes it works. This time it doesn't. Mal starts squirming and his shrieks get impossibly louder. For a ten-year-old kid, Mal is incredibly strong—it's all I can do to hang on.

Mom appears in the bedroom doorway with the rug. The instant Mal sees the rug, I feel him relax.

The rug is eight feet long and three feet wide. It looks like the carpet in a movie theater: about a dozen colors all mixed and scrambled together in a random-looking pattern designed to hide soda-pop stains and trampled Junior Mints. In fact, that's exactly what it is—an end scrap of some ugly commercial carpeting. Dad got it from one of his clients and brought it home to use in front of his workbench in the garage, only he never got to do that because Mal fell in love with it, and what Mal loves to do is roll himself up.

Mom lays the rug out on the floor. I slowly ease my grip on Mal.

"Okay, Mal. It's burrito time." I let go completely. He slides off the bed and lies down on the end of the rug, and I roll him up, all the way, his legs sticking out of one end, his shoulders and head poking out the other.

Mal closes his eyes and smiles. Being wrapped in the rug is the best way we've found to calm Mal down when he goes off. He'll stay there happily for a time, a Mal burrito, then suddenly—it could be five minutes or an hour—he'll start whining and whimpering, and if somebody doesn't unroll him right away, he'll go right back to the screeching. It's all about the timing.

"Can you stay with him, David?" Mom asks.

< 28 >

I nod. I can tell from the dreamy smile on Mal's face that he's settled in for at least half an hour, so I sit on his bed and try—as I've tried many times before—to decode his Wall.

It's not just a random mass of feathers and leaves and butterfly wings. Mal has a system. I've figured out a few things. For example, all the yellow poplar leaves are stuck on with the stems pointing down, while the oak leaves point either left or right. The blue-jay feathers go every which way, but they're always underlined by a black feather from a starling or grackle. The brown feathers seemed to be randomly arranged, but I suspect there's a pattern I just can't see. Same with the butterfly wings, although I notice that the orange-and-black monarch wings are usually next to an oak leaf.

A few weeks ago, just to see what he would do, I went into Mal's room while he was outside, carefully removed two of the leaves and switched their positions. A few minutes later, Mal came back, looked at his Wall, and froze. I braced myself for an eruption, but he just turned his face toward me without meeting my eyes, smiled his lopsided Mal smile, went directly to the two leaves I'd moved, and put them back where they belonged.

Mal doesn't really talk, but he seems to know what we're saying sometimes. The words are there in his head, tumbling around, rearranging themselves and mixing with all the other data that comes in through his senses. I think his Wall is his way of talking back. If only we could figure it out.

One time Mom tried to get him to eat a bowl of chicken alphabet soup, the kind where the noodles are shaped like letters. Mal was fascinated. He picked a bunch of the letters out of his soup and lined them up on the edge of the table. Then he grabbed the box of Ritz crackers and took it back to his room without ever tasting the soup.

He had laid out the letters like this:

TWIFEKY   OCDRGP

I looked at those letters for a long time, thinking maybe it was some sort of secret code. In fact, I was so sure it was a message that I copied down the letters before I cleared the table. Later, I figured it out. The letters on the left were all made of straight lines. The letters on the right had curves.

Mal's no secret-code genius. But for a kid who doesn't even talk, I thought it was pretty clever what he did with those letters.

I look at him, all wrapped up snug in his rug.

He opens his mouth and says, "Okay."

I said that Mal doesn't talk, but technically that's not true. He has one word, and that word is "Okay." It can

< 30 >

mean anything: yes, no, help, go away, more, shut up, or any number of other things. In this case, I know it means he's ready to be unburritoed.

"You ready, bro?"

"Okay."

I unroll him slowly, talking the whole time—stuff like, *Hey, Mal, how you doing, buddy? You have a nice little rug rest? Here you go, just two more turns and I'll have you out of there.* . . . Mom says we should talk to Mal as much as we can. She says, "When Mal starts talking, we want him to know lots of words, not just 'Okay.'"

When Mal starts talking.

Mom is convinced that it will happen any day now. She says it's not uncommon. She reads everything, and there are lots of cases of kids who never speak a word until age four, five, six, seven . . . even ten. Not very many wait till they're ten, but Mom knows about the ones who do, and she's sure Mal is going to be one of them.

Mal is free. He hops up and walks out of the room and down the stairs, probably on the prowl for more chips. I listen until I hear Mom say something to him, then go back to my room to check BuyBuy. I tap a key to refresh the screen image . . . and I stop breathing.

The current bid for Jooky Garafalo's half hot dog is one thousand nine hundred ninety dollars.

My shoulders sag, and I slowly let the air out of my lungs. I'm out of the running. Probably just as well.

Bing! The counter advances to an even two thousand.

Who is crazy enough to pay two grand for half a Jooky dog? I'm about to sign off when one little detail catches my eye.

That can't be right, I think.

YOUR BID:
$2,000.00

Your bid? Meaning *my* bid?

Impossible! I gape at the screen, willing it to return to some semblance of reality.

Nothing. Shakily, I check my AutoBuyBuy settings. The maximum bid was set at two thousand dollars.

What?

I quickly cancel AutoBuyBuy, but the bid remains on the screen.

Decimal points are the worst invention in the history of the world. If not for decimal points we wouldn't have the Colt .45 revolver, Windows 8.1, or BuyBuy.com. A simple little mistyped decimal point is the difference between twenty dollars and two thousand dollars. According to BuyBuy, that was what I typed in as my maximum bid.

I wait, heart pounding, for the other bidder to top my $2,000 bid.

Please, please, please!

Nothing.

I sit there until midnight, when a big flashing rectangle appears on my screen.

CONGRATULATIONS! YOU WIN!!!

($2,000.00 has been charged to your credit card.)

I am the proud owner of the world's most expensive half hot dog.

< 33 >

‹ 7 ›

PICKLES

I don't sleep so good that night. Actually, I can't get to
sleep at all. At two in the morning, I call BuyBuy's customer service number and talk to a woman named Sue. I
think their headquarters must be in India or Singapore or
someplace where it isn't the middle of the night, because
Sue has an accent and she seems way too perky for two in
the morning. She keeps repeating the phrases "integrity of
the auction environment" and "your credit card has been
charged," and "terms of service agreement," all of which
add up to "You're stuck with your purchase."

Then she says, "But you can put the item back on
BuyBuy and sell it to someone else."

Problem solved!

Ten minutes later, with Sue's help, Jooky's half dog

is back up on BuyBuy with an opening bid of $10 and a "reserve" of $1,990, meaning that I'm not obligated to accept the final bid if it isn't at least $1,990. Sue says the ten-dollar opening bid is the best way to attract serious buyers. At Sue's suggestion, we set the auction to expire at midnight on Saturday. That will give other bidders five days to go at it.

I try to go to sleep after that, but it's no good. I keep getting up to check BuyBuy. But nothing is happening. *Maybe the other bidder went to bed,* I tell myself. *Maybe he'll see it tomorrow.*

I try to distract myself by rereading my Walking Dead comics, but I'm not in the mood. Eventually I slip into a fitful sleep. When I wake up, Mom is yelling for me to get Mal and come down to breakfast. I wake up my computer and sign on to BuyBuy.

Nothing. Not even one single bid.

I help Mal get dressed and escort him downstairs. Dad is sitting at the table, eating his usual breakfast of poached eggs, wheat toast, and orange juice. I didn't even hear him come home last night.

"Hey champ," he says, looking from me to Mal. "How's my boy doing this morning?"

"Mal's fine," I say.

Mal sits in his usual place. A bowl of Cheerios is

waiting for him. As always, Mom has put out a carton of milk and a spoon. Mal, as always, ignores them. He prefers to eat his Cheerios dry, one at a time, with his fingers.

"I hear Bridgette stopped by last night with her young man," Dad says.

"Yeah. We got a lesson in water-buffalo cheese."

Dad gives me a questioning look, but does not ask me to elaborate. He rarely does.

"Where's Mom?" I ask.

"She left just a moment ago. Your sister forgot her pen kit here last night, so Mom's driving it over to her."

Bridgette is crazy about her pens. Fountain pens, felt-tips, and rollerballs in every color you could imagine. She's been pen crazy ever since I can remember. Also crazy in other ways.

"Mom's driving thirty miles just to bring her a box full of pens?"

"That's right."

"That's nuts."

"You know how your sister gets." He eats the rest of his breakfast as I root through the fridge. I find a foil-wrapped slice of pizza balanced on top of a pickle jar. I pop it in the toaster and eat pickles while I'm waiting for it to heat up.

"Really, champ?" Dad says. "Pickles for breakfast?"

"And pizza," I say through a mouthful of pickle.

He shakes his head, drinks the last of his orange juice,

< 36 >

and looks at his watch. "I have to run to the office to meet a client." He stands up. "You're on."

By "You're on," he means that I'm responsible for baby-sitting Mal until Mom gets back from her oh-so-important pen-delivery mission.

"I have plans," I say, although the only plan I have is to sit in front of my computer and wait for somebody to bid on the Jooky dog.

"Mom will be back in less than an hour," he says as he lifts the top half of his suit from the hanger by the door. "I'm sure whatever you have going can wait."

"Right," I say. "Because nothing I do could possibly be important."

He stops moving for a moment, then slowly slips into his suit coat.

"I did not mean to imply that your time is not valuable," he says. "But my meeting is important. I'm sorry if it inconveniences you." There is more than a hint of sarcasm there. I brace myself for a lecture about how hard he works, and how important his job is, and how I'm not paying any of the bills in this household, but he lets me off easy. "Are we good?" he says.

For a fraction of a second, I almost tell him that I just charged two thousand dollars on Mom's credit card for half a hot dog. But I hold my tongue.

"We're *okay*," I say.

"Okay," Mal says, smiling, his cheeks distended with dry Cheerios.

After Dad leaves I tell Mal about the hot dog, and the two grand I put on Mom's card.

"I'll be grounded for eternity," I say.

Mal stares out through the patio doors leading to the backyard. He won't look at me when I'm looking at him. He never does.

"Okay," he says.

"So we'll get to spend lots of time together." I don't know if he understands me. I never do.

"Okay."

"Or maybe they'll send me off to military school and I won't see you for years."

"Okay."

"Not okay, Mal."

Mal pushes out his lower lip and looks down. He understands *Not okay*.

"But don't worry. I'm going to figure something out."

"Okay," he mutters at his lap. Now I feel bad because I've made him unhappy.

"You want to go out back and look for Things?"

He perks up at that.

"First you have to brush your teeth and stuff."

Mal's morning bathroom routine takes him about half

< 38 >

an hour. It took a few years, but Mal is now a master of personal hygiene. He hasn't had to wear a diaper since he was seven.

It's been a windy morning, so lots of new leaves have blown in over our six-foot privacy fence. I leave Mal in the backyard to hunt for treasures while I go back to my room to check my BuyBuy page. No bids. Just to get things started, I try to bid ten dollars, but the system won't let me bid on my own item.

I can sit there miserably and try to imagine the conversation I will eventually have with my parents. Or I can try to figure out a way out of this mess. Dad likes to say, *For every problem there is a solution*. Usually he says it when he can't figure something out.

One time I tried to argue with him.

"Aren't some problems unsolvable?" I asked. "What if I get run over by a truck and die?"

"Then you're dead, and you have no problem," he said.

⟨ 8 ⟩

GUMMY WORMS

"You should seriously grow a beard," I say to HeyMan.

We're sitting in his room eating gummy worms and looking at my BuyBuy page on his laptop. I don't know why, but whenever I do something massively stupid I just have to tell somebody. I told Mal what I did, but I don't get a lot back from Mal, so I needed to tell somebody who would understand just how monumentally stupid the stupid thing I did was. That's what best friends are for.

"I tried," HeyMan says. "My mom says she doesn't want to live with a Sasquatch."

"Maybe she'd be okay with a beard if you, like, shaved your head."

"Why would she be okay with *that*?"

"It's a trade-off, same as when she said you could get your ear pierced if you got an A in History."

HeyMan's hand goes to his earring, a little silver loop. He's ridiculously proud of it. But I think he's more proud of his A in History.

"I don't think she'll go for it."

"Why not? It's the same amount of hair, just on a different part of your head."

"I think she's anti-beard."

"But it's the principle," I say.

HeyMan shakes his head and gestures toward the screen. "So what are you gonna do about the Jooky dog? It's kind of looking like you own it."

"If I can't sell it—and it's not looking good—I have to come up with the money before my mom gets her Visa bill. I was hoping you might lend it to me."

HeyMan laughs. "Like I'd do that even if I *had* two grand."

"Thanks a lot," I say.

"You're welcome."

"Okay, how about you get the bidding started. Bid fifteen bucks. I'll pay you back."

"I'd need a credit card for that."

"You can't borrow your mom's?"

"I'd rather not. I mean, look how that worked out for you."

We both stare at the screen.

"What about Cyn?" he says.

< 41 >

"Cyn has a credit card?"

"No. But maybe she can hack one off the Web."

"Yeah, right." Cyn probably could, but there's no way I'd ask her to do that. "I don't think I want her to know about this."

"Why not?"

"She'll think I'm stupid."

"You've known her forever," HeyMan says. "You think she doesn't know how stupid we are?"

"True," I say. Compared to Cyn, we're both morons. I don't know why she hangs out with us.

HeyMan says, "She's gonna find out sooner or later."

"Let's make it later."

"So what are you gonna do?"

"If nobody buys the half dog I'll have to come up with the two grand."

"Yeah, right. How?"

"I have twenty bucks. I could invest in lottery tickets."

HeyMan regards me doubtfully. "And when you don't win? You got a backup plan?"

"Get hit by a truck?"

I'm not really thinking about stepping in front of a truck. Although it *would* solve my problem. I wasn't serious about the lottery, either. I need a better plan.

For every problem there is a solution. It's just a matter of finding it.

I walk home. Mom is in the front yard working on her peonies. She asks me to go check on Mal. It's automatic. She says it a hundred times a day. I check on Mal. He's attaching a new feather to his wall. I go back to my computer and check my BuyBuy page again. No bids. I do a search for "How can I make $2,000 quick?"

There are a lot of ideas online for making fast money. Most of them are sarcastic, illegal, or disgusting. One of the more reasonable suggestions is "Make big money! Sell your old junk on BuyBuy."

I look around at my old junk. My computer is four years old and worth maybe two hundred dollars. I have a ten-year-old copy of X-Men that might be worth five bucks, and I could probably get thirty bucks for my Walking Dead comics. I have an MP3 player worth twenty or thirty, and a hand-me-down phone worth nothing. My bike might bring fifty. I continue my old-junk inventory and come up with $419.92. My total worth.

⟨ 9 ⟩

SooperSlider

I'm thinking about pretending I've gone insane. I mean, even insaner than bidding on half of a hot dog. Like kidnapped-by-aliens insane, or believing-in-fairies insane. What can they do? Put me in an asylum for a few weeks?

I'm considering this when the house phone rings. I answer it automatically, even though I don't want to talk to anyone. I immediately wish I'd checked the caller ID. It's Derek.

"Dude," he says. Like we're friends.

"Bridgette's not here," I tell him.

"I know! I called to talk to you."

Like I should be ecstatic about that. But I *am* curious.

"What's up?" I say.

"Was that true what you said? About eating a pizza in four minutes?"

"Four minutes and thirty-six seconds," I say.

"How are you on SooperSliders?" he asks.

"Why?"

"How many SooperSliders do you think you can eat in five minutes?" he asks.

"I don't know . . . a lot?"

"How many could you eat for two hundred dollars?"

I think for a moment.

"*Really* a lot," I say.

Derek, in addition to all his other irritating qualities, is a member of the Kappa Alpha Delta fraternity at Simpson College. A fraternity, as near as I can tell, is just a bunch of college guys living in a big messy house having parties, and Derek's summer job is to stay at the frat house as a caretaker and fix the place up: repairing holes in the walls, painting, taking care of the landscaping, and making sure the rooms are ready for next year. Anyway, Derek tells me that his fraternity is having a summer fund-raiser for the Childhood Leukemia Center. It's an annual event, and most of the frat boys return to campus for the occasion. The main event is a slider-eating contest with a first prize of two hundred dollars. Last year the winner was a guy named Hoover who ate twenty SooperSliders in five minutes. The runner-up only managed to eat fifteen.

"You think you could down more than twenty?"
Derek asks.

"Easy," I say, with considerably more confidence than
I feel.

"Are you sure? 'Cause here's the thing—it costs
twenty bucks to enter, and there'll be a lot of big eaters in
the running, including Hoover."

"I can do it."

"How about we do a trial run? I'll bring over some
sliders tonight and we'll time you."

"Fine with me," I say. I like SooperSliders. "You
buying?"

"I'll buy. But you have to pay your own way into the
contest, okay?"

"Deal," I say. Twenty bucks to win two hundred
sounds like a good deal.

"I'll be over at seven with the sliders. You might want
to skip dinner."

"Right," I say.

Mom makes grilled cheese sandwiches and a salad for dinner. I am not big on salads, but I eat two sandwiches, some
of Mal's potato chips, and a few lettuce leaves to make my
mom happy. I almost ask her to make me another grilled
cheese, but then I remember Derek and the sliders.

• • •

I'm glad I ate, because Derek doesn't show up until almost nine. He is carrying a bag emblazoned with the SooperSlider logo: a toothy, disombodied mouth biting into a juicy, dripping slider.

Mom answers the door. She looks past him, puzzled.

"Where's Bridgette?" she asks.

"She's studying. I came to see David." He holds up the bag.

"What on earth is that?"

"SooperSliders," Derek says.

"Those little hamburgers? That's very thoughtful of you, Derek, but we've already eaten."

"They're for David."

"We're doing an experiment," I say, coming up behind her.

Mom looks from Derek to me, then shakes her head.

"I don't know where you put it," she says.

We set up at the kitchen table: four rows of five sliders. I lift the top bun off one of them and look at it. SooperSliders are not grilled like a normal hamburger, they are steamed. The meat isn't crispy and dark; it's more of a pallid gray and only about a quarter of an inch thick. I put the top of the bun back in place.

"I hope you're hungry," Derek says.

"I'm always hungry." Looking at the rows of sliders

on the table, I wish I hadn't eaten that second grilled cheese.

Out of the corner of my eye I see Mal peeking into the kitchen. I don't say anything. Mal likes to pretend he is invisible.

Derek takes out his phone and brings up the stopwatch app. "Let me know when you're ready."

I grab the biggest glass in the cupboard and fill it with water.

"How many did that guy Hoover eat?"

"Twenty."

"In five minutes?"

"Yeah."

I take a deep breath and let it out slowly.

"I can do this."

"Go!"

The first slider goes down in three bites. I'm chomping into the second one before it reaches my stomach. I demolish number three in two bites and follow it with a quick gulp of water. I'm on number five when Derek says, "One minute."

That's a good pace, but I can do better. I smash the next five burgers flat to get the air out of them and start shoving them in one after another, a train of smooshed sliders. I drink more water and start on the next row.

"Two minutes," Derek says.

The slider train is slowing—there's a traffic jam just south of my breastbone. I see Mal standing just behind my right shoulder. Every time I get a burger down, he is silently mouthing the word "Okay."

I stand and jump up and down—that's called the Joey Jump, Joey Chestnut's trademark move. The traffic jam loosens. I grab a slider and eat it while I'm jumping.

I hear Mal's voice: "Okay, okay, okay."

I sit and keep shoveling, going to a two-handed technique. *Squish, bite, swallow, squish, bite, swallow, squish, bite, gulp water, squish, bite, gulp . . .* In the background I hear Mal going "Okay, okay, okay" over my shoulder to the sounds of me biting and breathing and gulping.

"Okay," Mal says.

I am in the zone. The next minute is a blur, and suddenly I am holding the last burger in my right hand, and it is moving toward my mouth in what feels like slow motion. I open wide; the slider enters the gate; my jaws close. *Bite. Bite. Bite.* I move the pulverized slider back in my mouth and open my throat and feel it ooze down my gullet to join its friends.

"Okay," Mal says. He turns and walks away.

I look at Derek. "How'd I do?" My voice sounds weird, like I'm talking from inside a barrel.

"Twenty sliders in three minutes and thirty-nine seconds," he says. "Pretty good. You think you could eat more?"

My belly is as taut as an overinflated basketball.

"Easy," I say.

"Dude, we are golden!"

I don't feel golden. "'Scuse me," I say. I stand up—not quite straight up. I'm not sure what is about to happen, but I figure the best place to find out is the bathroom.

I make it, just in time.

‹ 10 ›
FRITOS

The day of the fund-raiser, I tell my mom that I won't be home for dinner because I'm going over to Simpson with Derek.

"He's going to give me a tour of the campus. I graduate high school in four years, you know."

She gives me a long, searching look. "I'm glad you're thinking about college so early, David, but . . . a tour? At night?"

"Well, it's not a tour, exactly. They're having a fund-raiser at his fraternity. It's twenty dollars for all you can eat."

"Hmm," she says, making her concerned face. "I don't suppose it's all the beer you can drink, too?"

"Don't worry. I'm not gonna drink."

"What about Derek? I don't want him driving you home if he's drinking."

"I'll make sure he doesn't."

I can tell she's looking for a reason to tell me not to go.

She fails. "Well, I guess you're old enough to not do anything stupid."

We both know *that's* not true.

During the drive to the college, Derek expounds upon his philosophy of life.

"Everybody is good at something," he says. "Take me, for example. I am good at recognizing opportunities and capitalizing on them."

"Such as?" I am already bored.

"Such as today. If I hadn't taken the *opportunity* to give you the *opportunity* to enter this contest, you'd never have had the *opportunity* to win it."

"That's a lot of opportunities."

"It's what I'm good at," he says. "You're good at eating. Did you know you're basically a tube?"

"I'm a what?"

"A tube. Teeth on one end, butt hole on the other. All those other things—arms, legs, eyes, brain, heart—are just extras. Topologically speaking, you're a meat donut—a hole surrounded by flesh. If you take into account the nostrils, you are a three-hole donut. But basically you're a tube."

"Great. Now I feel really special."

"I'm a tube, too. It's important to recognize one's own nature."

Derek reaches into the backseat and grabs a snack-size bag of Fritos. He tears it open; the car instantly fills with the smell of corn chips. He shoves a handful into his mouth and starts chewing and talking at the same time.

"Did you know that Fritos were invented in the nineteen thirties?" he says.

I didn't know that, but I want some. I make a move toward the bag, but Derek holds it away from me.

"The only thing you're eating today is sliders."

"Thanks a lot."

"Just stay hungry," he says, munching. "So what do you do when you're not eating?"

I do a lot, I want to say, but instead I say, "Nothing."

"You don't have a girlfriend?"

"I'm fourteen," I say. "I haven't had the *opportunity*."

"Sometimes you have to create your own opportunity."

"There's not a lot of choice in Vacaville. I mean, there are only about twenty girls in my whole class."

"What about your friend the Chinese girl?"

"You mean Cyn? She's not—"

"She's cute. She got a boyfriend?"

"No. And she's not—"

"Opportunity," Derek says.

"Cyn's just a friend," I say. "And she's not Chinese. She's Korean-American."

"Whatever." He shrugs. "Same thing."

It's a good thing Cyn isn't there, because she might have taken the *opportunity* to punch him in the throat.

< 54 >

‹ 11 ›
POSSUM

The Kappa Alpha Delta frat house looks nice from the outside: three stories, ivy-covered brick walls, little peaked windows sticking out from the slate roof, and a fresh coat of white paint on the wraparound porch.

"You *live* here?" I say.

"Officially, yeah. But sometimes I stay with Bridgette." He gives me a look. "Don't tell your folks."

I have a conflicted moment—it's kind of cool to be in on Derek and Bridgette's secret, but it feels yucky at the same time. I don't say anything.

Inside, the frat house is more like a pigsty. The main room is littered with beer cans and crumpled snack-food bags, the tile floor is sticky, and the oversize stone fireplace has been used as a trash bin.

"I thought your job was to fix the place up," I say.

"No point in doing much until the fund-raiser's over—they'd just trash it all over again."

A guy wearing boxer shorts and a Simpson College sweatshirt appears from another room and sees us standing there. He salutes Derek with his beer, slopping foam over the rim of his plastic cup, and screams, "DUDE!"

Derek returns the salute with a pretend beer of his own.

"I guess they got started early," Derek says.

"It looks more like a beer party than a fund-raiser," I say.

"It's both," Derek says. "We call it a fund-raiser and give some money to the cancer kids. That way the cops and the administration leave us alone. Also, we get free product from SooperSlider. Come on—everybody will be out back."

He ushers me through an even stickier-floored kitchen, where two girls wearing tank tops and gym shorts are serving loose-meat sandwiches on sesame buns. If you don't live in Iowa, you probably never heard of a loose-meat sandwich. It's like a sloppy joe, only without the sauce.

Derek says to one of the girls, "Hey, Britt, you seen Randolph?"

"Out back." She offers us each a sandwich. Derek takes one for himself but slaps my hand away when I reach for one of my own.

"Not for you."

Britt gives me a pitying look. "Gluten intolerance?"

"Contestant," Derek says.

If the inside of the frat house was a sty, the backyard is a zoo. About forty guys and a dozen girls are milling around, most of them clustered around a beer keg, all of them holding red plastic cups. Along the back of the trampled lawn several wooden doors have been placed on sawhorses to make a single long table. A couple of guys are setting up a row of folding chairs along the back side of the table.

Derek exchanges high fives with several of his fraternity brothers as we weave our way through the throng. Nobody pays any attention to me. Randolph, who turns out to be a weaselly-looking guy wearing a Deathchain T-shirt and a magenta fauxhawk, is in the side yard, standing over a charcoal brazier, turning some sort of animal on a spit. The smell of barbecued meat sets my mouth to watering. I take a closer look at the spitted creature and notice a long, naked, charred tail coming off one end of it. Suddenly I am not so hungry.

"Hey Derek," Randolph says. "Who's the kid?"

"This is David, Bridgette's little brother. He thinks he can eat fast."

"Has he met Hoover?"

"Not yet."

"He's kind of small, don't you think?"

"Yeah, but he's got a big mouth."

"Well, if he's got twenty bucks, we got sliders coming."

I hand Randolph a twenty—pretty much all the money I have in the world.

Randolph pockets the bill. "You're in. We got sixteen guys signed up. And one girl."

"Who?"

"Who do you think? Ally Boudreaux."

"Oh." Derek looks at me. "Ally came in second last year."

"What *is* that?" I ask, pointing at the thing cooking on the spit.

"What does it look like?" Randolph says.

"A giant rat?"

He laughs. "Close. It's a fresh Iowa possum."

I take a step back. Opossum is one of the things I won't eat. Not that I've ever considered it before.

"Possy was our mascot," Derek says. "She got hit by a car."

I try not to gag. Roadkill is another thing I won't eat.

"She'll be ready by the time the sliders get here," Randolph says.

Derek abandons me to talk to some of his friends. I find a relatively quiet corner in what used to be a garden, sit on a cracked stone bench, and watch the action. Mostly, the action is drinking beer and talking loud, so it's kind of boring. I keep thinking about the loose-meat sandwiches the girls were making. I sometimes think I have mental powers, because just then this guy comes walking up to me holding a paper plate piled with three loose-meats in one hand while using his other hand to shove a fourth one into his mouth. The guy looks like the Incredible Hulk, only not so green.

"Crazy party, huh?" he says.

"Yeah, I guess." I notice that he is wearing a holster strapped to his waist. It's not a gun holster—this holster is a cup holder clasping a plastic beer cup. He sets the plate of sandwiches on the bench, draws his beer like it's a six-gun, drains it, belches, and reholsters the empty cup.

"You hungry?" He points at the sandwich plate.

I *am* hungry, but I know I shouldn't eat anything. Not if I want to win two hundred dollars.

"No thanks," I say.

"They're really good."

"They look good. But I'm in the contest."

He laughs. "Me too!" He grabs one of the sandwiches and gestures at the plate. "I'll leave those for you." He walks off, eating.

I look at the two loose-meat sandwiches. My hand twitches and moves toward the plate.

"I see you met Hoover."

I jerk my hand back. Derek is standing in front of me.

"That was Hoover?"

Derek looks at the sandwiches and says, "How many of those did you eat?"

"Nine," I say.

"Seriously?"

"Don't worry. I didn't eat any," I say.

"Good. Because—"

He is interrupted by a horn. Several horns. Vuvuzelas, actually—those long, plastic horns people blow at soccer games. Everybody looks toward the sound as six vuvuzela blowers decked out in red-and-yellow T-shirts come marching into the backyard carrying stacks of red-and-yellow cardboard boxes emblazoned with the SooperSlider logo.

The SooperSlider team heads straight for the long table and starts setting out the boxes. Two of them unroll a gigantic plastic SooperSlider banner and fasten it to the edge of the table. They go back out to their truck and return with huge trays of SooperSlider wings, onion rings, and jalapeño poppers, then start handing them out to the crowd. My mouth is watering, but with Derek standing next to me, I can't have any.

"Eaters!" Randolph's voice booms from the speakers set up at each end of the long table. I see him off to the side, holding a microphone. "Take your places!"

"We're on," Derek says. He grabs my arm and pulls me

toward the table. Several guys, most of them enormous, are already taking their seats. I grab a seat near the middle. In front of each seat is an open box of thirty SooperSliders and a forty-ounce SooperSlurp. Randolph is talking, but I hardly hear what he's saying—I'm too excited. I see a girl sit a couple seats down from me. That must be Ally. She's not that big.

A voice in my ear growls, "How'd you like them loose-meats?" It's Hoover, grinning.

"They were awesome," I said. "I ate two more."

"That makes us almost even." He takes the seat next to me and belches. "I ate six."

Randolph is still talking. ". . . new rule this year, gentlemen and lady. In honor of our late mascot, Possy, every contestant will start out with a scrumptious possum appetizer!"

The two girls who were making the loose-meat sandwiches move down the table, presenting each of us with a small paper plate containing a chunk of spit-roasted road-kill opossum.

"I thought this was a slider-eating contest," I say, scowling down at the bloody, undercooked hunk of Possy flesh.

Hoover grins at me. "Man, I love me some possum!"

I turn to Derek, who is standing behind me. "Do I have to eat this?"

He shrugs, looking worried as Randolph answers my question over the loudspeakers: "Time starts when I say go. Possum must be consumed before you get into the sliders. ARE YOU READY?"

"YEAH!" yells everybody but me.

"GO!"

I watch with horror as Hoover shoves his hunk of possum meat into his wide mouth, chomps down twice, and swallows.

"David! Go!" Derek yells in my ear.

I take a deep breath and fill my mouth with possum. I can't bear to chew it, so I force it to the back of my throat and swallow. It gets stuck. I grab my SooperSlurp and guzzle. The possum meat breaks loose, and I get it down. I take a quick look at Hoover. He's already on his third slider.

"Go!" Derek shouts.

I go.

The slowest part is the unwrapping. When I did my practice run with Derek, we unwrapped all the sliders ahead of time. I tear into my box with both hands—rip off wrapper, squeeze slider, shove, chomp, swallow. *Rip-squeeze-shove-chomp-swallow.* By the time I get half a dozen down I have a system for unwrapping with one hand as the other hand shoves. I peek at Hoover. With all the loose wrappers on the table it's hard to tell, but I think he's about five ahead of me. I try dipping the squeezed slider in my SooperSlurp cup to facilitate the slide. It helps.

I hear, in the distance, Randolph's amplified voice. "Two minutes!"

"Go!" Derek yells.

The crowd is chanting, "Hoo-VER! Hoo-VER!"

I think I'm on number twelve when I hit the zone. The sound of the crowd fades, and Randolph's announcements sound like the distant tweeting of a bird. The loudest sound is that of sixteen eaters chomping, gulping, gasping, and occasionally gagging. I stay in the zone. I shove them in, one after another, a continuous rope of pulverized slider from my hand to my stomach. I feel like everything is happening in slow motion. I'm afraid to look at Hoover—the sound of his eating is like the ocean in my left ear.

Suddenly, my box of sliders is completely empty. I look around in a panic. Now what? Hoover is staring at me, aghast. There are still three unwrapped sliders in his box. Everybody is looking at me. None of the other eaters have managed to finish even half.

I reach over to Hoover's box, take a slider, unwrap it slowly, and take a bite.

"Time!" Randolph yells.

The crowd goes wild.

People are thumping me on the back and shaking my hand. I am trying not to throw up. Randolph grabs my arm and pulls me to my feet.

"We have a winner—the Amazing . . ." He moves the mike away from his mouth. "What's your name, kid?"

"David," I manage to say.

"The Amazing David!" He screams into the mike. "David and Goliath!"

There is more cheering. Even Goliath—I mean, Hoover—is clapping.

With a flourish, Randolph presents me with a small plastic card. I look at it, not understanding.

Randolph throws his arm around me and squeezes. I almost lose it. "A TWO-HUNDRED-DOLLAR SOOPER-SLIDER GIFT CARD!" he shrieks.

More cheering.

I am in shock. I am beyond shock.

A *gift* card?

< 64 >

‹ 12 ›

CHEERIO

"That was *epic*," Derek says, for probably the tenth time. *"Epic."*

We are driving home in his little Toyota. I never before noticed how many bumps there are on the highway. Every time we hit a little crease in the asphalt, I can feel the jolt shivering the drum-tight walls of my stomach.

Derek gives me a concerned look.

"You gonna hurl?"

I slide my butt forward on the seat to straighten out my abdomen a little.

"I can pull over anytime," he says.

I shake my head and close my eyes. Bad idea. I open my eyes and swallow.

"You okay?" Derek says.

"Gift card," I mutter.

"Hey, I didn't say it was for cash. Besides, you like SooperSliders, don't you?"

"I need money."

"Tell you what, I'll buy the card off you."

He reaches into his breast pocket and pulls out a thick wad of bills. "I made a few side bets," he says.

I regard the wad of bills with mixed feelings. "How much you win?"

"A couple hundred."

"Okay," I say, and reach for the money. He pulls it back. "I didn't say I was gonna give you all of it. Tell you what, I'll give you fifty bucks for the card."

If we hadn't been going sixty miles per hour, I'd have shoved him out of the car.

"Forget it," I say. Maybe I can sell it on BuyBuy.

He shrugs and puts the money back in his pocket. "Whatever."

It's almost ten by the time Derek drops me off at home. I manage to stagger from the car to the house without barfing. My mom is in the living room watching TV. Arfie is sleeping at her feet. They both look up. Mom says, "Did you see Bridgette?"

"Nope." I sink slowly into my dad's recliner and stretch out. "Where's Mal?" I ask, because we are always supposed to know where Mal is.

"Dad took him for a drive." Mal likes to ride in cars.

"I won the contest," I say.

"Contest?"

"At the fund-raiser. They had a SooperSlider-eating contest. I ate thirty in five minutes."

"David!"

"Then I ate one more. It wasn't that hard."

"David, that's disgusting."

"It was, kind of." The mass of grease and meat in my belly is churning. "But I won two hundred dollars."

She looks away. "You *could* make money doing something useful."

"Like what?"

She shakes her head, and I feel a little sicker. I lever myself out of the recliner and slowly make my way up the stairs. I can feel her eyes on my back.

No one has bid on the Jooky dog.

I lie on my back on my bed and watch the ceiling. There used to be a bunch of interesting cracks up there, but Dad and I plastered and painted it last fall, and now it is just an expanse of smooth off-white. It looks like mayonnaise. The world record for mayonnaise eating is four quarts in eight minutes. I close my eyes and imagine the river of pulverized slider crawling sluggishly through my digestive system.

My situation is seriously desperate, and I'm not talking about the sliders in my gut. Sometime in the next few weeks, an envelope will arrive in the mail, and it will contain my mother's Visa bill, and there will be a two-thousand-dollar charge from BuyBuy, and life as I know it will come to an end.

My phone chirps.

I sit up with a groan. It's a text from HeyMan.

> How did you do?

I type in my reply.

> I won.

Two hundred dollars' worth of SooperSliders. The thought of eating another slider produces an alarming gurgle in my upper intestine. I hit SEND, turn off my phone, and flop back on the bed. A few minutes later, I hear the front screen door slam. Dad and Mal are back. I hear Mal's feet on the stairs. I close my eyes. My bedroom door opens. I pretend to be asleep. I know Mal is standing in the doorway. All he wants is for me to look at him and say good night, but I just can't deal with him at the moment. Sometimes Mal feels like a huge ball and chain. Sometimes I wish he didn't exist.

< 68 >

I hear him coming closer, and I sense him standing over me. Something touches my lip. I jerk my head back and open my eyes to see Mal's hand, offering me a single Cheerio.

"No thank you, Mal." I pull the covers over my head.

A few seconds later, I hear him shuffle out of the room and close the door behind him.

I feel terrible.

PEANUT BUTTER AND BANANA

The next morning I wake up feeling pretty good—until I remember my Jooky-dog situation. Still no bids. I go downstairs. Dad is sitting at the kitchen table, drinking coffee and reading a trade magazine about refrigerators.

"Mal's still in bed," he says. "Mom is at yoga."

"What about Bridgette?" I say. "Where's Bridgette?"

He misses my sarcasm completely.

"She's at school, I imagine, getting straight A's," he says.

"I'm in the kitchen," I say, "pouring a glass of orange juice."

"I'm in the kitchen too, having a conversation with my son. Arfie is sleeping on the sofa. The sun is in the sky." Maybe he gets it after all.

"Dad, what if I needed to make a couple thousand bucks this summer?"

"You are not buying a motorcycle," he says.

"Why do you think I want a motorcycle?" I ask.

He shrugs. "That's what I wanted when I was your age."

"Suppose I want the money for something not a motorcycle. How could I do that?"

"Get a job," he says.

"How am I supposed to do that? I'm fourteen."

"Deliver papers, mow lawns, run errands . . . I don't know. Why do you need money? We give you ten dollars a week."

"That's, like, one pizza," I say.

"How many pizzas do you need?"

"That's not the point."

"Well, I'm sure if you put your mind to it, you'll figure something out. For every problem there is a solution."

I *knew* he was going to say that.

Summer jobs for underage teens in Vacaville are in short supply, as in zero. Billy Fisher has the neighborhood lawn mowing sewed up, and Alison Keller delivers the *Vacaville Voice,* our local paper, which hardly anybody subscribes to anyway. I find nothing online except for pizza delivery, and you need to be able to drive a car for that.

Thinking about pizza makes me hungry, so I make myself a couple of peanut-butter-and-banana sandwiches.

Mom comes home from yoga and sees what I'm eating.

"I was planning tuna melts for dinner," she says.

"That sounds great," I say.

"It did before you ate the last of the bread."

"Oh. Sorry. I needed a snack."

"You always need a snack."

"Dad says I should get a job," I say.

That gets her attention. "He did?"

"To make some money," I say, as if there is any other reason to get a job.

"What about Mal?" she says. "I count on you being around most of the time in the summer. It's the only time I can get any work done."

"What work? You don't have a *job*."

I know the second the words come out of my mouth that I've made a mistake. Mom's eyes harden, and she starts listing all the things she does.

". . . cooking, shopping, paying bills . . ."

I pretend to listen. I've heard the list before.

". . . taking Mal to his therapy, keeping the house clean, volunteering at the food bank, helping your grandmother with her shopping and taking her to the hairdresser every week . . ."

It's a long list.

". . . neighborhood association meetings, putting together client mailings for your father, keeping the weeds from taking over the garden . . ."

"Okay, okay," I say. "I get it."

"I don't think you do!"

"I *do*. But what about my life? I have one, you know."

"You have plenty of free time. What have you been doing in your room all morning?"

"Actually, I was investigating job opportunities."

She closes her eyes and sighs. "What do you need money for?" she asks. "We give you money."

"That's, like, one visit to SooperSlider."

"We have food here. You're not starving. You don't need to eat thirty super-whatevers every day."

"A job would teach me responsibility," I say.

"You're very responsible already."

"I think it would be good for me. Just part-time. I can still help with Mal."

"Well . . . let me talk to Dad about it."

I figured that was about as far as I could push her. I put my plate in the sink.

"See you later," I say.

"Where are you going?" she asks.

"I don't know. Maybe over to HeyMan's."

"What about Mal?"

"What *about* him?"

"I have to go grocery shopping. We have no bread."

"I'll go," I say.

She gives me a measuring look, then nods slowly and takes a twenty-dollar bill from her purse. "We need bread, mayo—the large size—and orange juice, the kind your dad likes. And two boxes of Cheerios."

I take the twenty. "You sure this is enough?"

She sighs and gives me another twenty. "Get *two* loaves of bread. Something with whole wheat in it. And don't forget the Cheerios. And I expect some change, okay?"

"Okay," I say.

"Okay," says Mal. He is standing in the doorway, looking miserable. He's taken off his T-shirt and attempted to put it back on, but he's somehow managed to get his head through the armhole.

"Good look, Mal," I say.

Mom clucks her tongue and goes to help him. I make my escape before she can expand the grocery list. On the way out, I check the mailbox. A couple of catalogs and the electric bill. I'm going to have to keep a close eye on the mail from now on. Maybe I can buy myself some time if I intercept Mom's Visa bill.

Four Seasons Market is on the outskirts of fabulous downtown Vacaville, a ten-minute walk from home. I decide to take a stroll through downtown on the chance that I might find a Help Wanted sign in one of the businesses. Unlike a lot of other towns in Iowa, Vacaville has a thriving business district, with four restaurants, an old-fashioned movie theater, a couple of bars, a good assortment of retail stores, and a twenty-foot-tall fiberglass cow named Vaccie.

Vaccie is located in the exact center of downtown on her own grassy meadow. The meadow is really a traffic island about fifty feet across located at the intersection of Main Street and First Avenue. Maybe you've heard about her. Vaccie is listed in several travel guides, is featured on travel websites, and has been written up in the *New York Times*. People come from miles away to take pictures of Vaccie, the Pride of Vacaville.

Today, the only company Vaccie has is a guy in coveralls applying a fresh coat of pink paint to her udder. Tourists like to take pictures of themselves reaching up and "milking" Vaccie. It wears the paint off, so every year her udder gets a fresh new coat.

I walk up and down Main and the parallel side streets, but the only employment opportunities I see are for a hairdresser at Krazy Kurlz and the more-or-less permanent sign in the window of Pigorino Pizza: DRIVERS WANTED.

Being in the vicinity of Pigorino's makes me forget that I just ate. My stomach and my feet carry me off the sidewalk and into the restaurant. *Just one slice*, I tell myself.

The smell of baking pizza hits me like a truck, and

< 75 >

the next thing I know I'm ordering a medium combo with extra sausage and cheese. As I'm waiting, I notice a new poster on the wall next to the cash register. The poster shows an American flag, an Italian flag, and images of pizza slices floating around between the words.

My heart starts pounding as I read the words on the poster. I squeeze my eyes closed, open them, and read the poster again.

Super Pigorino Bowl
The World's Greatest Pizza Eating Contest
GRAND PRIZE $5,000
Iowa State Fairgrounds
August 15th

Problem solved.

< 76 >

‹ 14 ›

Extra Sausage and Cheese

I never dreamed that Papa Pigorino would actually do it.

A few months ago, I was sitting in a booth waiting for a pizza when Papa Pigorino himself walked in the door.

"Hey Papa," I said.

He looked at me and spread his arms and grinned.

"Doug!" he said.

"It's David," I said.

"David! My favorite-a customer! How-a you-a doing?"

Everybody is Papa Pigorino's "favorite-a customer." Papa is a born salesman. He calls himself the Colonel Sanders of pizza, and he looks the part, right down to the white three-piece suit and the pointy little beard. Except his beard is black, and he's only about five foot two, and instead of a tie he wears a heavy gold chain that he adds a link to every time he opens a new restaurant. There are twenty-three Pigorino's, mostly in Iowa, plus one in Chicago and two in Omaha. But the Pigorino's in downtown Vacaville is the original, and I've known Papa since I was a little kid—even if he doesn't always remember my name.

"I'm doing good, Papa," I said. "How about you?"

"We all-a got-a our-a problems." He stroked his gold chain. "Business no so good."

Two other things about Papa Pigorino: (1) he loves to complain about business, even though he sells tens of thousands of pizzas every week, and (2) his Italian accent is totally fake. Papa Pigorino's real name is Elwood Gronseth. He grew up on a hog farm ten miles south of town.

"People no eat-a the pizza like-a they-a used to. Too many crazy diets."

"Have you heard of the pizza diet?" I asked.

That got his attention. "Pizza diet? I like!"

"No crust, no meat, no cheese."

"I no like."

"Me neither. Hey, you know what you should do? Have a contest!"

"Contest?"

"Yeah, like Nathan's Famous hot dogs. They get all kinds of advertising with their hot-dog-eating contest. And they sell more hot dogs than *anybody*!"

"That's-a good-a for them."

< 78 >

"You could do it with pizza. Whoever eats the most slices in ten minutes wins."

Papa got this faraway look in his eyes. "Papa Pigorino, he is a-liking this-a idea."

"It's a great idea," I said, not so modestly.

I hadn't really expected anything to come of it, but now I'm looking at the poster and reading the small print. Every Pigorino's in the country—all twenty-three of them—is having a qualifier contest on the Fourth of July. There's no cash prize for the qualifier, but the winners will be entered in the Super Pigorino Bowl at the Iowa State Fair in Des Moines.

That's where the money is. But only the victor wins the five thousand dollars. Second prize is free pizza for a year. Third prize is a Papa Pigorino Signature Pizza Cutter. All participants will receive a Papa Pigorino T-shirt.

The entry fee for the qualifier is fifty dollars. I figure I can eat more than fifty dollars' worth of pizza, so that's a no-brainer. And I'm pretty sure I can eat faster than anybody else in Vacaville, so qualifying is a gimme.

I do the math: *no-brainer* plus *gimme* equals *the greatest opportunity of a lifetime*.

I'm rereading the poster for the tenth time when my pizza arrives. I take it to a booth and wait an eternity for it to cool. When I judge it to be a reasonable number of degrees below the temperature of hot lava, I set the timer on my phone and dive in.

Four minutes later, I call HeyMan.

"Three minutes forty seconds," I say when he answers.

"Is that some sort of code?" HeyMan asks.

"It's the David Miller World Record for scarfing an entire Pigorino's combo with extra sausage and cheese."

"No way," HeyMan says.

I tell him about the contest.

"Dude! You can't lose!"

"I'm not so sure about that," I say. "Last year, Jooky ate forty-two slices in ten minutes. That's, like, fifteen seconds a slice. My time is double that."

"Yeah, but you had extra sausage and cheese."

"True. But the really good news is that the Pigorino contest is on the Fourth of July. That's the day of the big Nathan's contest in New York. All the pros will be at Coney Island eating hot dogs. I need fifty bucks to enter, though. Can I borrow it?"

"Huh."

"What does *that* mean?"

I hear him say, not into the phone, "He wants me to give him fifty bucks for some pizza contest."

"Not *give*! *Lend!*" I shout. "Who are you talking to?"

"Cyn."

< 80 >

"Where are you?"

"At her house. I'm helping her put together a bookshelf—*ouch!*"

"What happened?"

"She threw a book at me. Um, I guess I should have said I'm *watching* her put up a bookshelf."

I hear Cyn's voice in the background. "Much better," she says.

I grab a Super Pigorino Bowl entry form on my way out of the pizzeria. The Fourth is only ten days away, and I have to pay my entry fee by Friday. I keep thinking about HeyMan and Cyn. It bugs me that they would be hanging out together without calling me, even if it's just to watch Cyn put up a bookshelf. Also, it bugs me that HeyMan is being weird about lending me the fifty bucks. I know he has it.

I'm thinking so hard I forget to do Mom's shopping until I'm almost home. I have to turn around and walk all the way back to Four Seasons. I get everything on the list—just barely, since the pizza took a big chunk out of the money Mom gave me.

She's in the kitchen when I get home.

"Did you get Cheerios?" she asks.

"I got everything." I plunk the bag on the counter.

She holds out a hand. "Change?"

I give the one dollar and seventeen cents I have left.

"That's all?" she says.

"I took my allowance a day early." Before she can respond to that, I say, "By the way, I decided I don't need a job."

"Oh?"

"Yeah. Pigorino's is having a pizza-eating contest. I'm going to win it."

"Absolutely not," she says.

My grin goes away. *"Why?"*

"People all over the world are going hungry. Those contests are a disgusting display of excess and gluttony."

"It's a *sport*," I say. "Dad always says I should do more sports."

"Eating is not a sport."

"It is if you can eat seventy hot dogs in ten minutes like Joey Chestnut."

She makes a *tsk* sound with her tongue, rolls her eyes, and slumps her shoulders—the whole I-can't-deal-with-this-right-now package.

"Go check on Mal," she says without looking at me.

⟨ 15 ⟩
SLIM JIM

The next morning I stick around the house until the mail comes, just in case there's a Visa bill to intercept. Later I'll head over to HeyMan's and try to pry fifty bucks out of him. I'm pretty sure if I get in his face, he'll lend it to me. The mail usually comes around ten, so I keep an eye out. As soon as I see the mail carrier coming up the block, I go outside and wait for her by the mailbox.

"Waiting for this?" she says, smiling. She hands me a thick nine-by-twelve envelope. It's from somebody named V. Schutlebecker.

V. Schutlebecker? For a moment I'm mystified. The return address is Rockford, Illinois. I don't know anybody in Rockford. Then I realize what it has to be. The Jooky dog! I've been so obsessed with worrying about Mom's next Visa bill I almost forgot about the half hot dog that started it all.

I sort quickly through the rest of the mail. No Visa bill. I dump the mail on the bureau in the front hall and run up to my room and tear open the package. Inside is a cheap black plastic frame containing a Certificate of Authenticity. I know it's a Certificate of Authenticity because it says

Certificate of Authenticity

across the top. Below that is a photo of Jooky Garafalo. He is smiling and holding half a hot dog. Beneath that, in fancy script, are the words

I, Jooky Garafalo, hereby certify that I did not eat this half hot dog.

I read it twice. Kind of a weird way to say it.

At the bottom, in blue ink, is Jooky's scrawled signature.

But where's the dog? I look in the envelope and see a wad of crumpled tissue paper at the bottom. I take it out and unroll the tissue and uncover a small, oblong object tightly wrapped in tinfoil. With shaking hands, I unwrap the foil. Inside is a dark, shriveled tube of protein nestled

< 84 >

in a shrunken, flattened, rock-hard, bone-dry bun. It looks more like a Slim Jim than a hot dog.

The Jooky dog is mummified.

I don't know what I expected. I knew it wouldn't be fresh and plump and edible—the contest was almost a year ago—but I thought it would look more like . . . like a hot dog.

I try to imagine this petrified relic on display in the State Historical Museum in Des Moines. What was I thinking? No wonder nobody's dumb enough to bid on it.

Nobody except me.

My first impulse is to share my idiocy with my best friend. I text HeyMan.

The Jooky dog has landed.

< 85 >

‹ 16 ›
MUSTARD

I'm heading up the walk toward HeyMan's front door when I hear voices and laughter coming from out back. I go around the house and look in the backyard. HeyMan is running across the lawn with a badminton racquet. He swings wildly and misses the birdie. On the other side of the net, Cyn is laughing. I stop at the corner of the house. HeyMan retrieves the birdie and hits it over to Cyn, who returns it in a high lob. I like watching her move.

I've mentioned that Cyn is tall, but I haven't said anything about the way that tallness is put together. She has mad pretzel abilities. When I met her back in the first grade, Cyn could put both feet behind her head and roll around in the grass like a ball. I bet she can still do it. She's not only flexible, she's incredibly graceful—watching her swing that racquet is like watching water flow.

HeyMan moves more like a gorilla. He staggers toward the birdie and hacks at it with his racquet, sending it into the net. They're both laughing. HeyMan isn't as clumsy as he is pretending to be. He knows he can't beat Cyn, so he's clowning around. He grabs the birdie, tosses it high in the air, takes a mighty cut at it, and misses.

Cyn notices me. "David!"

HeyMan looks up and for a moment I see disappointment on his face. It lasts only a fraction of a second; then he grins and salutes me with his racquet.

"SooperSlider Slim! The Sultan of Slide!"

Cyn ducks under the net, picks up the fallen birdie, and starts bouncing it on her racquet.

HeyMan points at the envelope in my hand. "Is that it?"

"Um . . . no," I say. I didn't know Cyn was going to be there, and I'm not sure I want her to know what an idiot I am.

"C'mon," HeyMan says. "Let's have a look." He makes a grab for it; I jerk it away and glance at Cyn. She is bouncing the birdie, pointedly not looking at us.

"I told her," HeyMan says.

"You did?" I shouldn't be surprised. HeyMan has a big mouth.

"I know all about your fabulous investment," Cyn says, still not looking at me. "Pretty dumb."

"Yeah, I know. Thanks."

"Are you gonna show it to us or not?" HeyMan says.

Reluctantly, I open the envelope and take out the Certificate of Authenticity. HeyMan and Cyn look it over.

"Where's the dog?" HeyMan says.

I remove the half dog from the envelope and unwrap it. The three of us stare down at the mummified thing.

"Wow," HeyMan says, poking at it with his forefinger. "It's even got a little smear of dried mustard on it."

"Careful," I say. "It's fragile."

"Did you really pay ten thousand dollars for it?" Cyn asks.

"*Two* thousand," I say.

She looks at HeyMan. "You told me ten!"

"So I exaggerated," he says, not looking the least bit embarrassed. "Any BuyBuy bids?"

"Not even one."

"That's kind of weird. You'd think whoever was bidding against you before would try again."

"Unless he doesn't know about it. Maybe he's on vacation or something."

"Didn't you wonder why the person you were bidding against stopped bidding at exactly nineteen hundred and ninety dollars?" Cyn asks.

In fact, I hadn't. "I guess I just assumed that the other guy limited himself to two thousand dollars. It's a nice round number. Unfortunately for me, I got there first."

"Still . . . kind of an odd coincidence," she says.

"She's right," says HeyMan. "What if the other guy bidding was actually the seller trying to jack the price up?"

"You can't bid on your own stuff. The site won't let you. I tried."

"Yeah, but don't forget—*you* asked *me* to bid it up for you. Maybe he had a partner."

"Um . . . yeah . . . but . . . there's no way the other bidder could know how high I was willing to go."

"Unless he hacked your computer," HeyMan says.

"Or hacked BuyBuy," Cyn says.

"That doesn't make sense," I say.

"Neither does paying two grand for a hot dog," HeyMan says.

We all contemplate that.

"Either way," I say after a moment, "if I can't come up with two grand, I'm dead."

"You gotta win that contest," HeyMan says.

"Yeah, but first I have to win the qualifier. And then I have to win the Pigorino Bowl in August."

"So what's the problem?" HeyMan says.

"For one thing, I need fifty bucks to enter the qualifier, and I'm pretty much broke."

"Oh," he says, taking a step back.

"I can lend you the money," Cyn says. HeyMan looks startled.

"Seriously? That would be great! Tell you what, if I win, I'll give you a cut."

"Oh, you don't have to do that," Cyn says, but I can tell she likes the idea.

"Ten percent," I say.

"Hey . . . what about *me*?" HeyMan says. "I got fifty bucks."

"Yesterday you said you didn't."

"Yesterday you said you wanted to *borrow* it. I have a policy against lending money to friends."

"No you don't."

"True. But yesterday I did."

"So now you want to lend me fifty bucks?"

"No! I want to *invest* it."

Cyn bops him on the top of his head with her badminton racquet. "My idea," she says.

"Can't we *both* invest?"

"He only needs fifty," Cyn says.

All of a sudden everybody wants to give me money. I say, "Look, I can sell some stuff if I have to. Hay's right. Borrowing money from friends is never a good idea."

"It's not *borrowing*, it's *investing*," HeyMan says.

"Either way, I have to think about it."

They both look at me, then at each other. Cyn shrugs and goes back to bouncing the birdie on her racquet. HeyMan looks hurt.

"I thought we were the Three Musketeers," he says.

I give him a few seconds to think about that, and then I say, "Okay. You can both invest fifty. Because I need money for training, too."

"Training?" HeyMan asks.

"Yeah. As in food."

< 91 >

‹ 17 ›

TWO PIZZAS

I stop by Pigorino's to pay my registration fee. Vito, who works the counter most days, takes my money and scrawls my name on a list posted on the wall behind him. I boost myself up onto the counter and lean forward to read the names of the other contestants. There are five of them so far. I know three of them. Jake Grossman is a Pigorino's regular and the nose tackle on the Vacaville High football team—a big guy who can demolish a sixteen-incher and have plenty of room left over. The twins Tim and Tommy Fangor are on the list—also big guys. The Fangor family owns a big dairy farm and creamery just south of town, where Papa Pigorino gets his mozzarella. I've never seen them eat, so who knows? The other two names are unfamiliar.

"Hey," Vito says, "get off my counter."

I slide back down. "I need a pizza, too," I say.

"You always need a pizza," he says.

"Make it two," I say. "Pepperoni."

It's time to start training in earnest.

I've never actually eaten two entire pizzas in one sitting before. As I sit in the booth and wait for them to cool, I try to figure out how many slices I can eat in ten minutes. A few days ago I managed to down one in under four minutes, but could I keep up that pace? Or improve on it? Joey Chestnut could average fifteen seconds a slice. . . . I do the math. At eight slices per pizza, Joey could demolish these two pies in four minutes.

I touch the center of one of the pizzas. Still too hot.

A stocky, older guy with a neatly trimmed gray beard is standing at the counter talking to Vito. He's wearing a new-looking John Deere feed cap and a pair of crisp dark denim overalls over a chambray shirt that looks as if it's been starched and pressed—a farmer all duded up in his go-to-town best.

My pizza is reasonably cool, so I set the timer on my phone, press start, and dig in. I eat the first slice normally: one big bite at the tip, then two more bites on either side, then turn the crust on end and devour it in three bites. I demolish the second slice in six bites, then take a gulp of water. For the third slice, I shift tactics, folding it with one hand and eating it in five bites. It goes down a little rough—the bottom of the crust is dry—so I switch to a reverse fold, with the cheese on the outside. Now I'm onto something.

Five, six, seven, eight slices. I peek at the timer. Two minutes, fifty seconds. I hit the second pie.

The first slice sticks halfway down. I have to gulp extra water, then stand up and do the Joey Chestnut jump, straight up, then land hard on my heels. Four jumps and it breaks free. I grab another slice and stay with the reverse-fold, bite, bite, bite, bite system.

I'm slowing down. My jaw hurts, and my hands feel as if I'm underwater. I press on, thinking, *Where's the zone?* In the slider contest, I hit the zone and became an eating automaton. Pizza is more technical—every bite is different.

Getting down the last slice is like eating a slab of greasy cardboard. I can hardly bear to chew it, and when I try to swallow, it stops at the back of my throat and refuses to budge. I stand up and do the Joey Jump, but it doesn't work—I have to cough it back into my mouth and chew it a few times and drink more water. Finally, after a few more Joey Jumps, it goes down. I check the timer.

Seven minutes and thirty-two seconds.

I sink back into my seat, feeling defeated.

"You got fast jaws, son."

I look up. The old guy in the coveralls is standing behind me.

"But you got to learn to pace yourself."

I try to say, *Yeah, right*, but all that comes out is a wet belch.

"The real champions, they come from behind," he says.

I want to say, *What do you know about it?* But that last slice is still oozing its way down my esophagus, and I don't want it to reverse course.

"Order up," Vito calls out.

"Don't worry, kid," the old guy says. "You'll get the hang of it." He goes to pick up his order and takes it to the booth across from me. I stay where I am, unable to move, and watch him carefully separate the slices of his plain cheese pizza, then get up and go to the restroom. He comes out a minute later, still drying his hands on a paper towel. He sits down and tucks a napkin in the collar of his neatly pressed shirt, looks over at me, and winks.

On an impulse, I reset the timer on my phone and wait for him to start eating. As soon as he lifts the first slice, I hit start.

At first he doesn't seem to be in a rush, chewing and swallowing each bite, dabbing his mouth with his napkin and sipping his coffee every slice. But there is a

< 95 >

machinelike regularity to his eating, an unhurried, graceful ballet of mass consumption. It's weirdly relaxing to watch. I don't take my eyes off him the entire time, and when he finishes the final slice, I am so entranced I almost forget to stop the timer. When I look at the number I can't believe it.

Three minutes flat. Only ten seconds longer than it took me to eat my first pizza, and he hadn't even been trying.

He sips his coffee with a satisfied smile, then takes out his wallet, leaves a tip on the table, and nods to me.

"Later, Vito," he says as he heads for the door.

"Who was that?" I ask Vito.

"Egon Belt." Vito jerks a thumb over his shoulder, pointing at the list on the wall. "He just registered for the qualifier."

My heart drops into my already-overfilled belly.

18

CABBAGE

Egon Belt!

You may not know who Egon Belt is, but I sure do. Ten years ago, Egon took fourth place at Nathan's. And he still holds the Deep-Fried Cheese Curd record: six pounds six ounces in ten minutes. But he hasn't been active lately—I figured he'd retired.

I sit there in the booth for a long time, thinking. Do I even have a chance? Belt is a pro—he's been eating fast since before I was born. And the way he ate that pizza, almost leisurely, without cramming slices into his mouth, without any fancy folding or dipping in water or doing the Joey Jump. How fast could he eat if he was really trying? My mind is boggled. There is no way I can beat him in the qualifier.

I stare at the pizza crumbs on the trays before me. I look over at the table where Egon Belt was sitting. Not a crumb.

But I beat him. I downed my first pizza in two minutes fifty. And mine was pepperoni. Belt's was plain cheese. *I can do this.*

"Hey." Vito is leaning over the counter, looking at me. "You okay?"

I nod. "I was just thinking . . . what's Egon Belt doing in Vacaville?"

"He lives over in Halibut."

Halibut is only ten miles away. I didn't know Egon Belt was from Iowa.

"He comes in every now and then," Vito says.

"He sure ate that pizza fast," I say.

Vito nods. "He'll probably win this thing."

I feel a spark of anger. "I ate my pepperoni faster than he ate his cheese," I say.

"Yeah, but you practically busted your jaw doing it. Egon wasn't even trying. I heard he ate ten pounds of cheese curds in six minutes."

"It was *six* pounds in *ten* minutes."

Vito shrugs. "Still, that's pretty impressive."

"Yeah, well, we'll see who's impressive."

Egon Belt might be bigger and more experienced, but I *need* to win. I slide out of the booth and stand up straight. Well, almost straight. There's a lot of half-chewed crust poking at me from inside. Vito says, "Hey, I forgot to give you this." He's holding out a sheet of paper.

The page is covered with small print.

"What's this?" I ask.

"A waiver. Since you're underage, you got to have one of your parents sign off on it."

Great. Another parental negotiation.

I've got a lot of work to do if I'm going to beat Egon Belt, and I have only nine days to do it. I think about going back inside and ordering another pizza, but my funds are limited, and I don't want to deal with Vito's negative energy. Besides, there are better things than pizza for increasing speed and stomach capacity. On my way home, I stop at Four Seasons and invest in some training materials.

The great Kobayashi trains by eating huge bunches of whole grapes. Joey Chestnut drinks gallons of water. Jooky Garafalo swears by iceberg lettuce. But from everything I've read online, the king of stomach-stretching is raw cabbage.

I dump the grocery bag on the kitchen counter. Mom is at her desk in the study, paying bills or something. I feel a twinge of guilt, even though her Visa bill hasn't shown up yet. I go upstairs to check on Mal. He is lying on his back across his bed, head hanging over the edge, snoring. I go to my room and wake up my laptop. No BuyBuy action. I open the manila envelope and take out the Jooky dog and the Certificate of Authenticity and stare at them, feeling like the biggest idiot on the planet. After a time, I put them back in the envelope and stuff it in a desk drawer and go downstairs.

Mom is standing at the counter, staring at the four heads of cabbage.

"That's a lot of cole slaw," she says.

"Mal's sleeping," I report.

"Your father hates cole slaw. Why did you bring all this cabbage home?"

"It was on sale," I said. "You don't have to eat any."

"Is this some sort of school project?" she says hopefully.

"Mom, school's been out for three weeks."

"You're planning to eat all this yourself?"

"I like cabbage," I say. I really don't.

She shakes her head and walks off. A few seconds later I hear the back screen door slam. She is going to work on her rose garden. That's one of the things she does when she doesn't want to deal.

I confront the cabbage. The outer leaves are kind of grody-looking. I peel them off, cut one of the cabbages into six wedges, sit down at the counter, and begin.

• • •

If you ever feel the desire to be completely and utterly miserable, I recommend two pizzas followed by an entire head of raw cabbage, eaten as quickly as possible.

Mom comes back in and finds me lying on my back on the floor. She looks at the cabbage shreds on the counter, then back down at me.

"Oh, David," she says. "What have you done?"

"Practice," I manage to gasp.

‹ 19 ›

SooperSack

The next day, I visit SooperSlider. I give my order to a towering, acne-speckled server. I think he's one of the guys on the Vacaville High basketball team.

"Two SooperSacks and two strawberry SooperSlurps, no ice," he repeats after me. "To go."

"Not to go," I say. "I'll eat them here."

He gapes at me, blinking. "Uh, you know that there are twenty-five sliders in a SooperSack, right?"

"Yeah, I know." I hand him my gift card.

It takes them ten minutes to fill my order. I carry the SooperSacks to a table, open the bags, and line up the sliders, five rows of ten. I set the timer on my phone. I feel like I'm sitting at Food Command Central.

Ready phasers.

Fire.

After my experience at Derek's fraternity, I'm practically a pro. I unwrap one slider with my left hand while shoving another into my mouth with the right. Almost immediately I find my rhythm. I am in the zone. I sense that people are watching, but I don't look at them. The sliders flow—I am a python swallowing a goat.

By the time I finish, ten minutes and six seconds later, a crowd of customers and SooperSlider employees has gathered around. Their reactions range from disgust to amazement. The manager, Mr. Dhoti, comes over and introduces himself. He is a short, spherical man wearing a red-and-white-striped SooperSlider tunic over a bright yellow shirt. He has a huge round bun-colored forehead, a double chin that hangs like a full hammock beneath his regular chin, and small features squished into the middle of his face. His head looks like a giant hamburger. He gives me a paper SooperSlider crown—what preschool kids who finish their meals usually get—and the crowd breaks into applause.

The SooperSliders do not produce the digestive-tract drama of raw cabbage, but I'm still pretty uncomfortable. Halfway home, which happens to be the miniature midtown meadow occupied by Vaccie the fiberglass cow, I have to stop and lie down on the grass. I call HeyMan.

"'Sup?" he says.

I groan, staring up at Vaccie's udder.

"Dude?"

"I can't move. Help."

"Where are you?"

"Under Vaccie's udder."

"I'm up at the Mall with Cyn and her mom." The Mall is an outlet store on the freeway, a few miles north of town. "Cyn helped me buy a shirt."

"Why?"

"She says I need a new look."

"You don't *have* a look."

"Well, I do now. Why can't you move?"

"I ate fifty sliders in ten minutes," I say.

"Dude! That's got to be a record!"

"It's not," I say. "Joey Chestnut did a hundred and three Krystals in eight minutes."

"What're Krystals?"

"Krystal burgers. They're like SooperSliders, only we don't have them in Iowa."

"Do you really need help?"

"Hang on." I roll over onto my hands and knees and slowly rise, grabbing one of Vaccie's teats to steady myself. Everything stays down. "I think I'm okay," I say.

"Good. I gotta go try this shirt on. I'll call you later."

"Later." I disconnect and stagger toward home, wondering what's going on with Hay and Cyn.

At least my training is going well.

FOAM RUBBER

My parents are officially Very Concerned.

When I got home from SooperSlider, I oozed upstairs and crawled into bed for three hours and refused to come down for dinner. Mom came upstairs and looked in on me to make sure I wasn't dead or something.

"I ate at SooperSlider," I said. "I'm not hungry."

She processed that, then said, "How much did you eat?"

I knew I should lie, but I was rather proud of my performance, so I told her—even though I could tell from her look of horror and disgust that it was a mistake.

An hour later, both of them, the Parental Duo, come up and sit down on either side of my bed and inform me that it is Time to Talk. I grab my extra pillow and hug it to my chest—I don't know why; it just feels good.

"Your mother," my dad says, "is Very Concerned about this Eating Thing."

"Eating Thing?" I repeat.

"This contest you want to enter."

"I'm already entered," I say.

"And look what it's doing to you. Fifty hamburgers? It's obscene!"

"And two SooperSlurps," I say.

They stare at me.

My father says, "David"—he compresses his lips, looks at my mother, and continues—"setting aside the fact that there are tens of millions of people who can't afford to eat, stuffing yourself that way can be hazardous to your health. Obesity, choking, esophageal tears, damage to your stomach and intestines, high cholesterol, a strain on your liver and kidneys, and who knows what else?"

"It's just a one-time thing," I say.

"One time? Yesterday you ate an entire head of cabbage!"

I decide not to mention that the cabbage was on top of two pizzas. "I just want to win this one contest. Well, two, actually—the qualifier on the Fourth, and then the Pigorino Bowl next month. I can do it!"

"There are lots of things you 'can do' that aren't advisable. You could probably eat that feather pillow you're holding, but that doesn't mean you should do it."

"It's not feathers. It's foam rubber," I say.

He sighs. "Why are you doing this, David?"

I *could* tell them that it's because I need the money to cover the Visa bill that's about to arrive, but I don't. Also, that's only part of the reason. The other part is that eating mass quantities fast is the only thing I'm really good at, and it feels great to be the best. When I'm chowing down, I don't think about Mal, or the Jooky dog, or the Visa bill. It's like when I'm eating, I'm totally focused and everything else goes away. Even right now, as full as I am, I wish I could dive into a bag of sliders so I wouldn't have to deal with all this parental concern.

"I don't know," I say. "I just do."

Surprisingly, he seems to accept that as a reasonable argument. But he's not done.

"How are you paying for all this food you're eating?"

I tell him about the SooperSlider gift card. "And I have some money saved up," I add. I don't tell them about Cyn and HeyMan being my investors. "Besides, when I win the Pigorino Bowl, I get five thousand dollars!"

"As I understand it, if you don't win, you get nothing."

"Second place is free pizzas for a year. That's three hundred sixty-five pizzas!"

My mom hasn't said anything yet, but she makes a face at this.

< 107 >

My dad says, "David . . . we are not going to forbid you from doing this. It's your money and your body. But I strongly suggest you consider using your time more productively. Weren't you thinking of taking a summer job?"

"Winning the contest *is* a job."

They look at each other like a creature with two heads regarding itself.

"Your mother and I were talking," he says. *Obviously,* I think. "You know you're a big help to us, taking care of Mal."

"Okay." That's Mal, standing in the doorway. His face is tight. Mal does not like it when we argue.

"It's okay, Mal," I say. "We're just talking."

He looks normal, like a kid who can talk for real, but he is staring hard at something invisible, something the rest of us can't see.

"What would you think of making Mal your job?" Dad says after a moment.

"Mal kind of *is* my job," I say. "He's all of our jobs. Except for Bridgette."

"I was thinking of something more formal, more . . . full-time. For pay."

"You want to pay me for taking care of my brother?"

"Just until school starts. Your mother could use a break."

"I'm thinking of taking a job myself," she says.

< 108 >

Startled, I say, "Huh?"

"Just for a few weeks," she says, suddenly animated. "I'll be teaching again. At a language camp up in Minnesota."

"Language camp? But . . . you don't speak any languages."

She laughs. "I speak English. I'll be teaching in an immersion program for immigrant teens. Kids from Mexico, China, the Middle East—everywhere! It's a tremendous opportunity. I've wanted to do something like this for a long time, but"— her eyes dart toward Mal, who is still standing in the doorway—"I haven't been able to."

I say, "Wait . . . you want me to stay home with Mal *all the time*?"

"Okay," Mal says.

"Not okay!" I try to imagine spending all day every day with Mal. I mean, I love him and he's my brother, but being around him for more than a couple of hours at a time makes me feel like one of the Things pinned to his Wall.

"It wouldn't be *all* the time," Dad says. "Just while I'm at work."

"But you work *all the time*!"

"I'll be cutting back a bit."

"It's only six weeks," Mom says.

"Six weeks! That's half the summer!"

"As I said, we'll be able to help you out with some spending money," Dad says.

< 109 >

I see what they're doing. I have stepped into that oldest of parental traps. First, they make me feel bad about wanting something, and then they give in, and then they hit me with the heavy-duty payback. Talk about being pinned to a wall.

I take a breath and let it out.

"How much does this job pay?" I ask.

Dad seems a little taken aback by that, but Mom smiles—she knows she's won.

"Er . . . twenty dollars?"

"An hour?"

"A day."

I pretend to think about it, but we all know I have no choice.

"Okay," I say. "But next Saturday is the qualifier at Pigorino's. The Fourth of July."

"My job doesn't start until the sixth," Mom says.

I make them wait a few seconds for my answer, then I say, "Okay, but I need you to sign something." I show them the waiver Vito gave me. Dad examines it, frowning.

"This says if you are injured during the contest we have no legal recourse."

"I won't get hurt," I say.

"Okay!" Mal yells.

We all turn to look at him. He is gripping the door frame with both hands and staring fiercely at the floor.

⟨ 21 ⟩

CRUST

The next morning, I don't wake up until after ten. I don't even check my BuyBuy page but go straight downstairs. Nobody's home. Mom must have taken Mal to therapy.

The waiver is sitting on the kitchen table. Dad signed it. I'm a bit surprised—last night he said he'd have to sleep on it, and that usually means *No*. But here it is. Mom must really want that job.

To celebrate, I eat the leftover lasagna from last night, let it settle for a few minutes, then head over to HeyMan's.

When I get there, the front door is standing wide open. That's not unusual in Vacaville. I walk inside. The little TV on the kitchen counter is on—some morning talk show. The sink is full of dishes. I can smell the remains of breakfast. I see a plate with three strips of cooked bacon on the table.

I yell for HeyMan. A second later I hear an answering croak from the back of the house. I grab the plate of bacon and head down the hall to HeyMan's room, munching on one of the bacon strips.

Hay's room smells like old sneakers. He's still in bed.

"Dude, it's eleven o'clock!"

"So?"

"So you're gross." I thrust the plate at him. "Have some bacon."

He eyes the two remaining strips of cold bacon, waves the plate away, and pulls the bedspread over his head. "Stop being so perky," he says in a muffled voice.

"I'm not perky." I sit at the foot of his bed and eat another piece of bacon. "How about pizza?"

He peeks out from the covers. "I just woke up. I haven't even had breakfast."

"Have them put a fried egg on top."

"You're serious," he says.

"I'm buying."

"Yeah, with *my* money!"

"Pigorino's opens at eleven thirty."

He sighs and throws the covers back. He's still wearing his jeans from yesterday. He grabs a random tee from the laundry basket on the floor, sniffs it, and pulls it on.

"Where's the new shirt?" I ask.

"I don't want to get pizza on it."

< 112 >

"Show me."

HeyMan opens his closet and takes out a dark-blue denim cowboy shirt with pearly snap buttons. LET'S RODEO is embroidered across the back in red and yellow thread.

I start laughing. I can't help it.

HeyMan scowls and shoves it back in the closet. "Cyn says it's *ironic*. I don't even know what that means."

I eat the last piece of bacon while he puts his shoes on.

By the time we get to Pigorino's it's after noon and I'm getting hungry. I order three cheese pizzas.

Vito says, "If you're that hungry, I could make you up a Grande BLD." He raises his eyebrows.

The Grande BLD is Pigorino's most insane pizza. It is to a regular pizza as a wedding cake is to a vanilla wafer. First, it's thick. *Really* thick. Stick your finger into a BLD and it will sink past not one but *two* knuckles before reaching the double-thick crust. There is red sauce, of course, but the sauce is not visible. It is covered by slabs of mozzarella and chunks of Iowa cheddar, followed by half a pound of Italian sausage nuggets, topped with a layer of pepperoni disks, then wedges of green and red bell pepper, mushrooms, sliced red onions, green and black olives, marinated artichoke hearts, and I don't know how many whole garlic cloves. Over that is a lattice of extra-thick bacon strips crowned by a nest of crispy hash browns containing an egg, sunny-side up, topped by a sprig of parsley.

It's a whole day's worth of meals in a single slice: Breakfast, Lunch, and Dinner.

I've *seen* the BLD, and I know what's in it because all that stuff is listed on the menu. I've never actually tried one. The BLD costs $39.95, and you have to order it an hour in advance.

"No thanks," I say.

Vito shrugs and writes down my order.

HeyMan orders a small bacon-and-cheese. "Since you ate all the bacon my mom left for me," he says.

We grab a booth and wait for our order. HeyMan is staring at his phone.

"What are you looking at?" I ask.

"The Heimlich maneuver. In case you choke."

"Nice to know you got my back."

The first pizza goes down fast. Two and a half minutes. Dipping the crust in water speeds things up a lot, even though it's kind of disgusting. Pizza number two goes almost as quickly: two minutes, forty-six seconds. But halfway through the third pizza, a chunk of hard crust turns sideways in my throat and just . . . stops. I can still breathe through my nose, but that crust is jammed in good.

< 114 >

I get up and do the jump. Nothing. I clench every muscle in my neck, I twist my head back and forth, I try to cough it back up, but it's wedged in like the Rock of Gibraltar.

HeyMan is looking worried.

"Dude, you choking?"

I shake my head. I grab a water glass and try to drink. Some of the water trickles past the crust, but some finds its way into my lungs. I cough, spraying flecks of half-chewed pizza. With a ferocious effort, I use my swallowing muscles to try to crush the crust. It feels like the sharp edges of the crust have burst through my esophagus, but the pressure eases; I feel it move. I do the Joey Jump again, three big jumps, landing hard on my heels. On the third jump, the crust crumbles and slides slowly toward my stomach.

I slide back into the booth and stare bleakly at the last four slices of pizza.

"You okay?" HeyMan asks again.

I nod. It hurts.

"You sure?"

I shrug. I don't feel okay at all. I pick up a slice of pizza, bite off the tip, chew it several times, then try to swallow. It feels like a hot poker being shoved down my throat. I hack it out—that hurts even worse—then close my eyes and slump back in the booth, defeated.

"David?" HeyMan says.

That's weird. HeyMan never uses my actual name. It would be like me calling him Hayden.

I touch my hand to my throat. Even that hurts.

"You okay?" HeyMan asks for the third or fourth time.

"Ghaak," I say. It sounds like a sob filtered through shards of glass. Feels that way, too. I look at HeyMan's face, at his bristly jaw, at the concern and confusion in his eyes, but mostly what I see is my future contracting down to a knot of shame and misery. I'm sure I've ripped my esophagus wide open and I'll have to spend the rest of my miserable life eating nothing but oatmeal and smoothies, and saying *Ghaak* because my voice box has been destroyed. I imagine sitting with Mal, having a conversation:

Ghaak.

Okay.

Ghaak.

Okay.

Ghaak.

"Drink something," HeyMan says, shoving his Coke across the table.

I take the cup and sip the ice-cold liquid. It feels good. I drink a little more.

"Thanks," I croak. I'm relieved that I can speak an actual word. I sip more Coke. The coldness feels good.

"You scared me," HeyMan says.

"Me too." My voice sounds better. "But I think I might've messed up my throat." Saying it out loud makes the possibility all too real.

HeyMan says, "You probably just ran out of room. I mean, you ate two and a half pizzas in six minutes."

"Six minutes? Really?"

"And twenty-six seconds."

That's even faster than I'd hoped. I swallow, and a wave of pain reminds me that I've just wrecked my esophagus, along with any chance I have to qualify for the Pigorino Bowl.

My life is over.

< 117 >

‹ 22 ›

ARTICHOKE AND PEPPER

My Jooky dog auction is over, too. I didn't get a single bid.

I curl up on my bed and squeeze my eyes closed and focus on my throbbing throat and feel sorry for myself. Any day now, my mom's Visa bill will arrive. My parents will never trust me again, and I'll be paying them back forever. They'll probably assign me to watch Mal full-time until I get out of high school. I imagine my mom's face, and my dad refusing to look at me, and Bridgette's smug, I-always-knew-you-were-a-loser expression. I just want to go to sleep and wake up in about ten years and have it all be different. But the way my head is buzzing, I'll never sleep again.

The mattress moves. I have company. Probably Arfie. In about one second, he'll be licking my ear, and I'll ignore him, and he'll go away.

Nothing happens. I reach out, expecting to encounter dog hair or a wet nose, but my hand hits fabric. I roll over and open my eyes.

Mal's face is about two inches from mine.

"Okay," he says.

I go back to my fetal position. "Go away, Mal."

"Okay," he says, but he does not go away. I sense him moving around; then he settles in beside me. I feel his warm breath on the back of my neck, and I know without looking that he has copied my position. We are like two flesh commas.

"I'm trying to sleep, Mal."

"Okay."

The next thing I know, Mom is yelling for us to come downstairs to dinner.

When we get downstairs, Mom is cutting up a pizza. I'd been hoping for soup or something easy to swallow.

"It's just the three of us tonight," she says cheerfully.

There is a bowl of dry Cheerios on the table. Mal sits down and immediately starts eating them with his hands.

Mom says, "Since you seem so determined to win that pizza contest, I thought you might like some practice."

"Oh . . . um . . . thanks." I pour myself a glass of milk and take a sip. To my surprise, it doesn't hurt to swallow. The nap must have helped.

"I really appreciate your agreeing to help out for the next few weeks, David."

She is being so bright and sunny, it's hurting my brain. I'm not used to it. It's as if going away from me and Mal and Dad is the best thing that's ever happened for her.

"Um . . . okay," I say.

"Okay," Mal says, spraying Cheerio crumbs.

"But you don't leave until *next* Sunday, right?"

"That's right. I'll still be here next Saturday, so you can go to your . . . what is it called?"

"Qualifier."

"Yes, qualifier." Mom puts the pizza on the table. "Eat up! This one's veggie, but I've got a pepperoni in the oven."

I pick up one of the smaller slices and take a small bite from the tip. I chew it several times, then slowly ease it toward the back of my mouth and swallow. It slides down with no problem. I sip my milk and try another bite. It feels *good*! It tastes good, too. I detect flavors of artichoke heart and green pepper. I eat more, taking care to chew it thoroughly and follow each bite with a sip of milk. Mom is watching me.

"I don't think I've ever seen you eat this slowly," she says.

"It's good," I say. I'm down to the crust. I want to skip the crust and start on another piece, but I've never done that before, so I bite into it and chew it for what feels like forever. The slight char gives it a bitter taste. There is something about that I like—a sort of cleansing after the gooeyness of the cheese and sauce, like a bottle brush for the digestive system. I swallow. Success! That first slice takes me almost five minutes to eat. It's the best slice of pizza ever. My throat feels fine, so I keep eating, picking up the pace as I go. Mom takes the second pizza out of the oven and cuts it up. I eat one slice of the pepperoni pizza, then stop.

Mom gives me a curious look.

"You don't like it?"

"No, it's great. I guess I'm just not very hungry tonight." I seem to be recovering from the crust disaster, but I don't want to take any chances.

"Are you sure? Do you want some ice cream for dessert?"

"Ice cream sounds great." At least I know it won't hurt my throat.

Mom puts a huge scoop of vanilla in a bowl. "Do you want some chocolate syrup on it?"

"Sure." It's crazy how nice she's being.

"Nuts?"

"No thanks. I'll take it smooth."

Mal has finished his Cheerios. He watches intently as Mom sets the bowl and spoon in front of me. Mal doesn't like eating cold things—he specializes in room-temperature food—but he is fascinated by ice cream. Not to eat, but to watch. I put a spoonful in his cereal bowl. As I eat my ice cream, he watches his dollop turn slowly into a white puddle. Have you ever watched ice cream melt? It's slightly more interesting than watching paint dry. Mal loves it.

< 122 >

⟨ 23 ⟩

YOGURT

I take the next day off. Yogurt and bananas for breakfast, and chicken noodle soup for lunch. Every top athlete needs an occasional day of rest, I reason. In less than a week, I'll be scarfing pizza like a demon, and I want to give my throat a chance to heal. It feels completely normal at the moment, but that thing with the crust really freaked me out.

I'm sitting at my computer reading about competitive eating records when I get a text from Cyn.

> Can u come over?

Cyn's house is one of the oldest in town, a three-story Victorian monstrosity with turrets on the two front corners and fancy carved cornices along the eaves. It was built by a wealthy grain merchant back in the 1920s, but when he died the home fell into disrepair. When I was a little kid it was boarded up, vacant, and called the Haunted House of Vacaville. Cyn's dad bought it and moved his family in when I was in the first grade. That's how long Cyn and I have been friends.

The Lees have been working on the house ever since. It's really nice now—it doesn't look haunted at all—but it's a big house, and there is still a lot of stuff to fix. When I get there Mr. Lee is at the top of a long ladder, wearing a dust mask and scraping a third-story window frame.

"Hey Mr. Lee," I call up to him.

He looks down at me and pulls his mask down onto his chin. "David," he says. "Did you stop by to help me scrape paint?"

"Looking for Cyn," I say.

"I thought as much. She and your friend Hayden are in her room performing some sort of computer wizardry. You can go on in." He pulls up his mask and goes back to scraping.

I walk inside and up the curving, carpeted staircase with a massive oak banister that Cyn and I used to slide down. It was fun until Cyn broke her arm. After that, Mr. Lee fastened some big wooden buttons along the top of the banister to keep us off it. HeyMan never got in on the banister-sliding because we didn't get to be friends with him until the fourth grade when he moved here from Des Moines.

Cyn's room is in one of the turrets. It's the only round room I've ever been in. She is sitting at her antique rolltop desk, typing on her computer. On the wall above her desk is a map of Korea, and next to the desk is a ceiling-high bookcase. Cyn reads books like I eat food. HeyMan is sprawled on the carpet reading an X-Men comic.

"What's up?" I ask.

"Cyn's been playing Nancy Drew," HeyMan says. He's wearing his ironic LET'S RODEO shirt.

"I found out who your Jooky-dog guy is," Cyn says. "Schutlebecker is an unusual name, and there's only one in Rockford, Illinois—Virgil B. Schutlebecker. So I cross-referenced the name with Jooky Garafalo and Nathan's Famous, and I came up with this guy." She turns her laptop toward me.

I recognize him instantly. Thinning blond hair down to his shoulders. Squinty, close-set blue eyes. And a smile that looks like it's been cut out of a toothpaste ad and pasted onto his face.

"That's El Gurgitator," I say.

"I know," Cyn says. "I've been reading about him. He doesn't exactly have a good reputation."

El Gurgitator—aka the Gurge—is the most infamous

< 125 >

eater on the circuit. He's won his share of contests and has been accused of cheating more than any other eater.

"The *Gurge* sold me the Jooky dog?"

"Well . . . he sold you *something*," Cyn says slowly.

"What's that supposed to mean?"

"Virgil Schutlebecker has a pretty active history on eBay," Cyn says. "He sells old comic books, souvenirs, all kinds of collectibles. His buyer-satisfaction rating on eBay is kind of lousy. That's probably why he's using BuyBuy now." Cyn raises her knees, wraps her long arms around her shins. And spins in her chair to face me. "I've been thinking. When we were looking at that hot dog, there was this yellow stuff on it."

"Yeah. It looks like mustard. So?"

"So who takes time to put mustard on a hot dog during an eating contest?"

I let that sink in, and the further it sinks, the sicker I feel.

I manage to say, "You think the Jooky dog is . . . *fake*?"

"Look at that face," HeyMan says, gesturing at the screen. "I wouldn't buy a dollar bill for a nickel from a guy like that."

"But how can it be fake?" I say. "It came with a Certificate of Authenticity!"

"I've been trying to track down Jooky Garafalo, too," Cyn says. "He's harder to find."

"Jooky's a mysterious guy. Jooky is probably just a nickname."

"His real name is Jeremy," Cyn says.

"How did you find that out?"

"I am a woman of mystery. But I can't find an e-mail or anything for him. He doesn't even have a website. I thought if we talked to him, we could find out if the Jooky dog is real. If we can prove it's fake, BuyBuy has a policy that says if you don't get what you paid for, you get your money back."

"I can get my money back?"

"If you can *prove* it."

"It has mustard on it!" I say, triumphant—but even as the words leave my mouth, I know that won't be enough. The Gurge would claim I put the mustard on myself, since one mummified half dog is pretty much like any other. Without Jooky, I'd have a hard time making my case.

Cyn and HeyMan are giving me equally pitying looks.

"I think I've been Gurged," I say.

⟨ 24 ⟩
CHEERIOS

The day before the qualifier, I have a dilemma: fast or gorge? Some of the stuff I've been reading online says that it's best to eat nothing the day before the contest. The theory is that if you're starving, food moves out of your stomach and into the intestines more quickly, providing additional capacity. But others say that you're better off continuing the stomach-stretching right up until a few hours before the event.

I have credit left on my SooperSlider card, a head of cabbage in the fridge, and enough money to buy several pizzas. I still haven't made up my mind whether to eat when I go downstairs for breakfast. Mal is at the table, eating Cheerios. Dad's gone. Mom is in her study doing something on her computer. I open the fridge and gaze sleepily at the shelves of food. I see yogurt and pickles and mustard and mayo and eggs and milk. No leftovers except some fish sticks from last night, and I can't deal with fish sticks for breakfast. I don't much like fish sticks anyway—just the name grosses me out. Mom makes them way too often, since it's the only form of protein Mal will eat. In the crisper drawer is cabbage, celery, carrots, and lettuce. Nothing looks good. There's a loaf of bread on the counter. I could make toast, but that doesn't sound good either.

I sit down across from Mal and pour some Cheerios from the open box into my palm. Mal freezes, staring at my handful of cereal. He takes a Cheerio from his bowl and puts it in his mouth. I imitate him, eating a single Cheerio from my hand.

We chew, me looking at Mal, Mal staring at my hand. Then we do it again.

I can see why Mal likes eating Cheerios this way. Each tiny crisp circle has its own special crunch and its own flavor profile: sweet, then sour, then a hint of salt and a sort of grainy, pasty, oaty aftertaste. I wonder what the world record is for eating Cheerios.

Mal and I eat Cheerios until the box is empty. He ventures a look at my face, smiles, then looks away quickly.

"Okay," he says.

• • •

< 129 >

I'm rewatching a Jooky Garafalo interview online from a couple of years ago. Jooky had just won a scrapple-eating contest in Pennsylvania. I have to look up *scrapple*. It's fried slabs of cornmeal and pork. Jooky ate nine pounds of it. That's a lot of scrapple.

"It's all about the flow, bro," Jooky says. "I get in this, like, Zen state of mind, and I, like, get my swallow muscles going in this slow-jam rhythm, man. It ain't nothin' without the flow. There's lots of guys faster than me, and guys with bigger stomachs, but if they ain't got the flow, I'm gonna waste 'em every time, 'cause I am, like, the Master of Flow."

Jooky is a cool-looking guy. He has a shaved head, several studs in his ears, and big aviator sunglasses, and he always wears a denim jacket with the sleeves cut off so you can see his tattooed arms. All his tats are fast-food logos: McDonald's, KFC, Chipotle, Sonic, Subway, and so on. He gets paid by the companies to display their logos.

"But you don't always win," the host pointed out. "Joey Chestnut beat you three years running at the Nathan's Famous event. Does he have the flow, too?"

"Joey, man, he's from another planet, another universe. Dude has, like, a black hole in his belly. Ain't nobody know where it go, bro. Another dimension, maybe."

"So you must have been relieved that he didn't enter the scrapple contest."

"Man, I don't care who enters what. I just love to eat. You feel me?"

Jooky is a class act.

I hear a metallic clank from downstairs and jump up. It's the sound of the mail slot. I go pounding down the stairs quick to get to it before my mom.

I'm too late. Mom is standing in the hall holding the mail as I skid to a stop in my stocking feet. She looks up. "David? Are you okay?"

"I'm fine," I say, desperately hoping the Visa bill isn't in there. "I just heard the mail come."

"Are you expecting something?"

"Not really."

"Well, it's probably nothing but bills." She drops the mail on the bureau. "I have to run out for a bit. Can you stay with Mal? He's in the backyard."

As soon as she leaves, I flip through the mail. Sure enough, one of them is the Visa bill. I put the mail back on the bureau, then nudge the Visa envelope toward the wall until it drops behind the bureau. I hear it hit the floor with a soft *tok*. The bureau is big and heavy, and nobody ever cleans behind it. If she does find it she'll assume it fell back there accidentally. By the time the next bill arrives I'll have won the Pigorino Bowl—I hope—and I'll be able to pay her the two thousand dollars.

It's not the best plan, but it's all I got. I turn away from the bureau and find Mal standing in the hallway watching me. He looks away. He's holding a long black feather, probably a tail feather from a grackle or crow.

"Tomorrow's the big day, Mal. Wish me luck."

He holds the feather in front of him and moves it back and forth as if he is a priest bestowing a blessing, then clomps up the stairs to add his new Thing to his Wall.

< 132 >

‹ 25 ›
PANCAKES

Saturday morning Bridgette shows up for breakfast and Mom makes pancakes. Bridgette is full of wonderful news. She got an A on her biology labs and a job promotion in the admissions office, and Derek *blah blah blah*. It's more interesting to watch Mal eat his Cheerios.

I skip the pancakes. Instead, I drink a half-gallon carton of apple juice. I want to take in enough to give my stomach a little stretch, but nothing that will stay there for long. The contest is at noon, and I'll need all that room for pizza.

Bridgette takes a break from her bragging to notice me. "Gross. Why are you drinking straight out of the carton?"

"To save on dishes," I say.

Bridgette looks at Mom, who smiles and shrugs.

"David's contest is today," she says, as if that makes it okay for me to drink out of the carton.

"You're letting him *do* that?"

"David is old enough to make his own decisions," she says, as if saying it will make it true.

I want to hug her, but of course I don't, because our family is not big on hugging. Except for when Mal starts shrieking; then we hug Mal.

"You should come," I say to Bridgette. "You might find it interesting."

"Derek told me about that thing at his fraternity. He said you were eating *roadkill*."

"Just one bite," I say.

Mom gives me a look, starts to say something, then clamps her mouth shut and gives her head a little shake.

"Competitive eating is a sport," I say. "If you knew anything about it you'd know that."

"I know it's disgusting," Bridgette says.

"It's just as much a sport as weight lifting or gymnastics. It's about pushing the limits of what the human body is capable of."

"Whatever," Bridgette says.

"You just hate it because I'm good at it," I say.

That takes her by surprise. "Why would you say that?"

"Because it's true. You have to be the best at everything."

"There are lots of things I'm not good at."

"Name one thing—besides eating—that I can do bet-ter than you."

She thinks for a moment. "You're better with Mal."

"Okay," Mal says.

"What else?" I say.

Bridgette looks at me blankly, as if she's never seen me before.

I say, "You don't actually know anything about me, do you?"

< 135 >

‹ 26 ›

BREAKFAST, LUNCH, AND DINNER

I meet HeyMan under the fiberglass cow. It's a hot, humid, windless day. We sit on the grass in the shadow of Vaccie's freshly painted udder.

"You know how many eaters are entered?" HeyMan asks.

"A dozen, last I checked."

The street is blocked off in front of Pigorino's. Some guys are setting up a long table on top of a low stage decorated with red, green, and white Italian flags. A big banner over the stage reads "First Annual Pigorino Bowl Qualifier" in alternating red and green letters. The smell of baking pizza permeates the muggy air. My stomach is making noises—I don't know if it's from being hungry or nervous. Or both.

"I wonder how many pizzas they'll make," HeyMan says.

"Well, I plan to eat four, at least. But I bet most of those guys won't make it through two."

"You worried about choking again?"

"That was a fluke," I say, hoping it's true. "I'll be dipping the crusts in water this time, going for maximum slide factor. Is Cyn coming?"

"She said she'd be here. Hey, here come the Fangors. Are they entered?" He points at a pair of identical blond hulks making their way down the sidewalk, followed by two blond girls, also identical. The Fangors have two sets of twins in their family. The girls, Tessa and Trina, are two years ahead of us in school and generally considered to be the hottest girls in Vacaville.

"Tim and Tommy are entered, but not the girls." I spot a familiar face. "See that guy in front of the drugstore?"

"The huge guy?"

"Yeah. He's from Derek's fraternity." I wave. "Hey Hoover!"

Hoover looks at us blankly, then recognizes me and makes a face. He crosses the street to join us.

"Hey kid," he says. "I was hoping you wouldn't be here."

"The contest was my idea," I say.

< 137 >

He barks out a sour laugh. "It would be. Oh well. I can always hope you choke."

"He choked last time he ate pizza," HeyMan says.

Hoover brightens. "So there's hope for me?"

"That was a fluke," I say.

"Just tell me Joey Chestnut ain't in town."

"Pretty sure he's at Coney Island right now for the Nathan's Famous contest," I say.

"Oh, that's today, huh?"

"Yeah, all the pros are in New York, so it's just us amateurs." I don't mention Egon Belt.

"So it's down to you and me then, huh? Clash of the Titans!"

"I guess."

Hoover heads over to where they're setting up the tables, and I see Cyn coming toward us. She waves and crosses the street.

"I have intelligence," she says.

"You don't have to brag about it," HeyMan says.

"I mean *intelligence* as in *information*. About your friend Virgil Schutlebecker."

"The Gurge is no friend of mine," I say.

"Yeah, well, he's no friend of a lot of people. I found a whole Reddit thread online full of Gurge haters. And that's not all. He also—"

Cyn is interrupted by a blast of feedback from the

stage. We look over and see Papa Pigorino himself stand-ing on the stage in front of a microphone.

"Contestants!" he shouts into the microphone. "All come-a to front-a of stage!"

"That's me." I run down the street to where the eaters are gathering in front of the stage.

Papa is strutting back and forth across the stage in his white suit with his fake accent, telling us-a he-a is-a proud-a to be-a here on this-a historic occasion. I see several familiar faces and a few strangers. Hoover is front and center, along with the Fangor twins. Jake Grossman, the biggest kid in my high school, is there, and so is Hap Hardwick, the football coach. Every single one of them is bigger than me, and they all look hungry. I see Egon Belt strolling unhurriedly toward us from down the block.

Papa is going over the rules, reading them from a long sheet of yellow paper. Pizza boxes may not be opened until the starting bell. Each pizza is cut into eight slices, and whoever finishes the most slices in ten minutes wins. The entire slice must be eaten to count—no tossing the crust. Chipmunking is allowed, but the contestant must swal-low whatever is in his mouth within sixty seconds after the final bell or be disqualified. A "Reversal of Fortune" is automatic disqualification. *Reversal of Fortune* is a nice way of saying *barf*.

I'm impressed with how thorough his list is. He's probably cribbed it from some other eating contest.

When he has finished reading the list, Papa looks at us and says, "Is-a that-a hokay?"

I raise my hand. "What about dipping?"

"Dipping?" Papa says.

"Can we dip the slices in our water?"

Papa is horrified. "Why you want-a to do-a that to Papa's nice-a crisp-a crust-a?"

"I don't know," I say, wishing I'd kept my mouth shut. I might've given away a pro tip to the other eaters.

"Whatever. Dip if you want to," Papa says, forgetting to use his fake accent. "Come on up—take your seats." As we all climb onto the stage and sit down behind the long table, Papa looks forlornly at the two dozen spectators. I'm sure he hoped for ten times that many.

Downtown Vacaville is usually a dead zone on the Fourth of July. There used to be an Independence Day parade, but not for the past few years. People are too busy doing other stuff—picnics, barbecues, and so forth—and they moved the fireworks display out to Vacaville Lake, two miles south of town. I think Papa was hoping his contest would lure people back.

Most of the spectators are friends and relatives of the eaters. I look for my personal cheering section, HeyMan and Cyn. HeyMan is right in front, chatting with the Fangor sisters with a silly grin on his face. A lot of guys get that way around Tessa and Trina. Cyn is standing a few feet behind HeyMan with her arms crossed, watching him with a carefully blank expression.

I end up sitting near the middle with the Fangor brothers towering on either side of me. I lean forward to check out the rest of the competition. Egon Belt is two seats to my right, then Hap Hardwick. They are the only two over thirty years old. I recognize the three other guys from around town but don't really know them. To my left is Jake Grossman, Hoover, and two more guys I don't know. Twelve of us altogether.

Vito is wheeling out the first batch of pizzas on a metal cart. He sets the boxes on the table in front of us, one box each. It's the extra-large box, not the sixteen-inchers I'm used to. That's fine with me—pizza is pizza. But why only one pizza each?

Vito goes back inside. I expect him to bring out more pizzas, but he returns with a tray of large plastic cups filled with water.

Hoover looks askance at the water. "No beer?" he asks.

"No-a beer," Papa says.

"No-a fair!" Hoover says.

Papa scowls at him. "No wise-a remarks or you-a disqualified."

That shuts Hoover up.

Papa looks over the spread and straightens out a few of the boxes.

"What happens when we finish this one?" I ask.

"You gonna eat more than one?" he asks, surprised.

"Joey Chestnut ate forty-five slices of Famiglia pizza in ten minutes," I say.

"You-a no Joey Chestnut," Papa says. "And this-a no Famiglia pizza."

"I'm pretty hungry," I say.

Papa considers this, then looks up and down the row of contestants.

"I'm-a pretty hungry too-a," Hoover says.

"You-a wise-a guy," Papa says. "You finish this one, we get you another."

More people have showed up. I don't know where they came from, but the crowd on the street has doubled in size.

Papa grabs the microphone. "Hokay, hokay, hokay! Is-a almost time for a big-a event! At this-a very moment, at Pigorino's all across the great state of Iowa, the world's greatest pizza eaters are sitting down to enjoy the world's greatest pizzas! One, and only one, of these amazing gladiators of the gut will go on to compete in the world's greatest pizza contest: the Pigorino Bowl!" He is so excited, he keeps forgetting his accent. "Let's have a big Vacaville welcome for our hungry contestants!"

He steps to the side, and everybody is looking at us and clapping. I see Cyn and HeyMan in front. They seem to be really close and really distant at the same time. I don't know if it's stage fright or excitement, but my heart is banging against my ribs and my hands are shaking and gravity has disappeared.

"ARE YOU READY?" Papa shouts into the mike.

Am I ready? I have no idea! The whole situation feels unreal, like I'm in someone else's body, in another reality. I want to say, *Wait! Hold on a second! Rewind!*

"GO!"

I open the pizza box. I'm expecting a cheese pizza, but what I find is something else entirely.

I am looking at a Grande BLD. Breakfast, Lunch, and Dinner. For a family of six. A two-and-a-half-inch-thick monstrosity supported by a double-thick crust turned up at the edges to form a tall, rock-hard rim. My throat hurts just to look at it. The pizza has been cut into eight fat wedges, then topped with a hash-brown nest big enough for a chicken, with a sunny-side-up egg and a sprig of parsley.

I look up and down the table. Most of the others are gaping at their BLDs in shock, uncertain how to attack, but Hoover has already picked up the fried potato nest in both hands, sucked down the egg, and is cramming the rest of it into his mouth, yolk running down his chin.

The rest of us dive in.

The potato nest is the easy part. I get it down in about twenty seconds, no problem, then pick up the first slice. It weighs a pound. I shove the tip into my mouth and bite down through the layer of bacon, vegetables, sausage, and crust. I don't bother tasting—all my energy is going into chewing. That crust is as thick as a slice of bread, but with the texture of baked cardboard. *Bite, bite, bite, swallow.* Again. My entire universe contracts. I am a biting and gulping machine. *Bite, bite, bite, swallow.* The rim is as hard as a week-old bagel. I dip it in my water glass and tear into it. Halfway through, I stop and tear the rim off the next slice and stick it in my water to presoak.

Egon Belt has finished his first slice and is munching contemplatively on his second, seemingly in no hurry at all. I look to my left. Hoover is on slice number two as well. The Fangors on either side of me are still struggling with their first slices.

I make quick work of slice two and power down the crust. The presoaking helps. I do the same thing with slice three.

"Five minutes!" Papa shouts into the mike.

I take another quick look at my competition. Some of them have already surrendered, but Egon Belt is a machine, already into slice four. Hoover and I are neck and neck, but I can tell from the redness of his face and the panicked look in his eyes that he is approaching the wall. I dive back in. I can feel myself hitting the zone. I forget about the other eaters and the crowd of onlookers. My entire universe is reduced to hands, mouth, teeth, and gullet. Time passes slowly. I don't even stand up to do the Joey Jump—my stomach has infinite capacity. My teeth blast through rock-hard crust; my throat opens and the pizza goes down.

Papa's amplified voice cuts through the fog of consumption: "One minute!"

I check out Hoover. He is starting his sixth slice, chewing frantically. Nobody else is even close to me and Egon Belt. The Fangors are regarding their remaining half pizzas blearily, making no effort to continue. Hap Hardwick has left the table. Jake Grossman is slumped morosely in his seat; he never made it past the third slice. I am on number seven. I can feel the pressure building inside.

Egon Belt is sitting back in his chair wearing a slight smile, his beard streaked with grease but still neat-looking. In the box before him rests a single slice of BLD.

I can catch up; I know it. I chew. I dip. I swallow.

I am shoving the last chunk of crust in my mouth when Papa shouts, "STOP!"

Egon Belt and I look at each other. I chew and swallow the last bit of pulverized crust. He winks.

It's a tie.

‹ 27 ›

VEGGIE PIZZA

The next few minutes are a blur. People are yelling and clapping, Papa Pigorino grabs my hand and Egon Belt's hand, and we both stand up. I just about lose it, but Egon Belt looks as if he's eaten nothing more than a donut and a cup of coffee. He's smiling and waving back at the crowd. Papa is yelling into his microphone. "Is a tie! Is a tie! We have-a two-a winners!"

He goes on, but I can't hear what he's saying—all I want is to get off that stage and lie down. After a few minutes that feel like hours, Papa runs out of things to say. I climb down off the podium, and HeyMan runs up to me and slaps me on the back. Seismic events occur within my digestive system. With a superhuman effort, I keep it together.

Vito is handing out free slices to the crowd. Just watching people shove pizza into their mouths is making my world spin. I stagger off toward Vaccie, toward that patch of shaded grass. HeyMan and Cyn, on either side of me, are both talking. HeyMan is telling me I'm awesome; Cyn is asking if I'm okay.

"I gotta lie down," I mumble. I sink onto the grass and stretch out. Cyn and HeyMan look down at me worriedly. I feel the BLD trying to sort itself out inside me. A few seconds later, Hoover joins us.

"I don't know how you do it, dude," he says with regretful admiration.

"Me neither," I say. I want to belch, but I think that might lead to other things.

"I thought that old dude had you smoked, but then he just stopped. You got lucky."

Egon Belt. I roll onto my side and push myself up, trying to stand without compressing my belly. Hoover grabs my hand and helps me up.

"Anyways, congrats," he says, then walks off.

HeyMan says, "Maybe you should, like, just not move for a while."

"I gotta say thanks."

"You're welcome," HeyMan says.

"I mean, to Egon Belt." I look around, trying to spot Egon Belt's John Deere cap. "Where'd he go?"

"I saw him go around back of Pigorino's," HeyMan says.

HeyMan and I find Egon Belt in the alley next to the restaurant sitting on an upended crate. He is sitting stiffly, leaning forward just a little, his big hands gripping his knees, his eyes fixed on something that isn't there. His face is unnaturally pale.

"Maybe we shouldn't bother him," HeyMan whispers.

Egon Belt must've heard him, because his head jerks up a notch and his eyes fix upon us.

I say, "Mr. Belt?"

"Yep," he says.

"Um . . . I just wanted to say thanks. You had me beat."

"That's okay," he says, following up with a small belch. "The rules say you got to eat the whole slice—half slices don't count. I couldn't have finished that last one anyway."

"Well, it was an honor to eat with you."

"Honor?" he says. I can hardly hear him. He squeezes his eyes shut for a few seconds. He really doesn't look good. His face is whiter than the inside of a hot-dog bun, and it's covered with tiny beads of sweat.

"It's no honor, son," he says after a moment. "It's gluttony and conceit."

< 148 >

He makes a noise that might be an attempt to laugh, but what comes out is another belch.

"But—"

"But nothing. Now, go on. Leave me alone." He swallows, looking paler than ever. The droplets of perspiration on his forehead are quivering, and I realize his whole body is shaking. "Go on. Get lost. Believe me, you don't want nothing to do with this business. And you do not want to be here for what's about to happen next."

I get what he is saying and start to back away. I can sense the pressure building. His face seems to swell, and the whiteness of it gives way to red as the blood rushes from his stomach into his extremities. HeyMan can see it, too. We turn our backs and walk quickly away. I flat-out refuse to describe the sound we heard a moment later.

Back in front, most of the spectators have left. Vito is moving the traffic cones off the street. Cyn is waiting for us in Vaccie's shadow.

"Did you find him?" she asks.

"Yeah," HeyMan says. "He's back there having a reverse-eating event."

Cyn grimaces, then looks at me. "How about you?"

"I'm okay," I say. "Things are settling down."

"I think they're still giving away pizza. You hungry?" She grins.

< 149 >

"Not so much."

"I guess there's a first time for everything."

"I think I need to go home and chill for a bit." I look back toward the alley. "I hope Egon's okay. He didn't look so good."

Just then, Egon Belt comes striding out of the alley. He goes over to Papa, who is helping Vito take down the folding tables, and shakes his hand. He's standing up straight, he's smiling, his color is normal, and his beard is neatly combed. He looks nothing like a guy who'd been barfing his guts out five minutes ago.

"Back from the dead," HeyMan says.

"Egon's a real pro," I say proudly.

< 150 >

‹ 28 ›
WORM

Mal is inching across the backyard on his hands and knees, his nose almost touching the ragged tips of the freshly mown blades of grass. He stops and picks up a withered dandelion blossom, examines it, then carefully sets it back in place. So far, the only Things he has kept are a single rose petal and a V-shaped twig, both now resting on the edge of the patio near the foot of the chaise longue where I have been sitting for the past hour.

Mal is inhumanly patient; I am inhumanly bored. Arfie, sprawled beneath the picnic table, looks bored, too.

I have a book, one of Dad's thrillers. Dad likes to read books in which large numbers of people are shot or blown up, especially stories that involve advanced military weaponry. In real life Dad is as peaceful as they come, but his taste in books is homicidal. The one I'm trying to read is about an ex-Marine whose wife is murdered by this secret government assassin group, and the guy sets out to kill them all, using a different weapon for each of them. I'm on page sixty-two, and so far there has been one strangulation, a drowning, a samurai-sword impaling, a machine-gunning, and two guys run over by a tank. Dad also likes politics, and there is a lot of politics in the book. I skip those parts. But the main reason I keep putting the book down is because of Mal. As boring as it is watching him crawl around in the grass, I can't stop watching. It's hypnotic.

My hypnotic trance is broken by the chirp of an arriving text message.

> **Sup?**

It's Cyn. I'm not in a texting mood, so I call her.

"Mal found a twig," I say.

"That's amazing," Cyn says. "Is it a good twig?"

"It is an excellent twig."

"Good for Mal."

"I'm reading about violent death and weapons of mass destruction."

"Why are you doing that?"

"It's one of my dad's books. I thought I'd give it a try. Did you know you can kill a man with a dessert spoon?"

"By feeding him too much pudding?"

"No, by—oh, never mind. It's stupid."

"I could have told you that."

"I'm watching Mal crawl all over the yard. It's very exciting. Really looking forward to the next few weeks."

"When does your mom get home?"

"The day before the Pigorino Bowl."

"How's your training going?"

"I'm taking a break." In fact, ever since the qualifier, every time I sit down to eat something, I remember the sound of Egon Belt barfing in the alley, and my appetite disappears. "You want to come over and help me watch Mal?"

"Only if he promises to find more twigs."

Twenty minutes later, Mal has collected a leaf that blew in from our neighbor's maple tree and another interesting twig. His knees and the palms of his hands are green from the grass, and he is getting that pinched look that happens when he is tired. I automatically go on meltdown alert.

"Hey." Cyn lets herself in through the back gate. "Any more twig action, Mal?"

Mal smiles and keeps his eyes on the ground. Very few

< 153 >

people can make Mal smile that way. He likes Cyn, but he won't look at her when she is looking at him. As soon as she looks away he senses it, and his eyes go back to her. Mal and I watch her cross the yard. Cyn walks like a cat, very smooth and liquid. I think that's why Mal likes her so much. He doesn't like people who move in jerks, or who stomp around, but he's liked Cyn ever since he was a toddler.

Cyn notices Mal's Things lined up on the edge of the patio.

"Good job, Mal," she says without a hint of sarcasm.

Mal gives no indication that he hears her, but I know he does. Cyn slides into the other chaise. "How are you doing?" she asks. "Are you nervous about the big contest?"

"I'll probably die of boredom before then, so not really."

Cyn smiles. "Mal isn't keeping you entertained?"

"You're lucky to be an only child."

"Why?"

"You get to be the oldest and the youngest all at the same time. I'm always stuck in the middle. I have a sister and a brother, but Bridgette's moved out, and even when she was here she treated me like a pesky rug rat. And Mal, well, look at him. It's like being alone with no privacy, you know what I mean?"

"Maybe you have middle-child syndrome."

"Is that really a thing?"

"No idea, but if it's not, it should be. Anyway, I wouldn't mind having a sister. Or even a brother."

"You want Mal?"

Cyn nods seriously. "I would take Mal. Is he for sale?"

We watch Mal. He has found something. It looks like a dried-up earthworm. Arfie, who has been watching from beneath the picnic table, trots over to investigate. Mal offers him the worm. Arfie sniffs it, turns away, and returns to his post. Mal replaces the worm in the grass and continues his crawl.

"Make me an offer," I say.

Cyn laughs, and I realize that this is the longest conversation we've had lately without HeyMan being there too. Just as I am having this thought I hear the gate open.

"Dude and dudette," HeyMan says cheerily.

I look at Cyn.

"I told him I was coming over," she says.

< 155 >

‹ 29 ›
GRILLED CHEESE

HeyMan wants me to eat more.

"You gotta stay in shape," he says.

"Or out of shape," Cyn says. She takes a bite of her sandwich. I made us grilled cheese sandwiches, just one each, and gave Mal a bowl of potato chips. He's sitting under the picnic table sharing them with Arfie.

HeyMan says, "You need to keep stretching your stomach. Here, have half of my sandwich."

"I'm not that hungry today."

"What's that got to do with it?"

I shrug. "I'm probably going to lose to Egon Belt anyway."

"No way! He's an old man. Besides, I have an investment in you."

"Maybe it was a bad investment."

"Don't say that! You took my money!"

"Okay, fine. You want out of the deal, I'll pay you back."

"With what?"

"I'll pay you back when I can."

"Yeah, in like ten years."

"Cut it out, Hay," Cyn says. "David will do his best." She looks at me. "Right?"

"Right."

HeyMan says, "Did you hear about your hero Jooky?"

"No. What?"

"He didn't even make the top five at the hot-dog contest."

I can't believe it—I haven't even looked up the results of the Nathan's Famous contest, and that was days ago.

"Jooky gave up after twenty dogs. He just stood up and walked off the stage."

"He must have been Gurged."

"The Gurge was a no-show."

"The Gurge got himself barred," Cyn says. "That's what I was going to tell you at the qualifier before I got interrupted. They caught him stuffing egg rolls in his pants."

"It's against the rules to put egg rolls in your pants at a hot-dog contest?" HeyMan asks.

"No! That was a couple weeks ago. At an egg-roll contest in Philadelphia."

"That sounds like the Gurge," I say. "Not that it does me any good." I think about the Visa bill behind the bureau in the hall.

Cyn, reading my mind, says, "Did your mom's credit-card bill come yet?"

I nod.

"What are you going to do?"

"Hide it until after the contest." Saying it out loud makes my plan sound even stupider. HeyMan and Cyn are giving me pitying looks again.

"Dude," HeyMan says, "you better start eating."

After Cyn and HeyMan leave, I follow Mal up to his room. He brings with him only the rose petal and the maple leaf—the twigs did not meet his standards. I leave him to his work and go downstairs to clean up the kitchen. Dad will be home soon; until then, I don't have much to do except keep an eye on Mal and contemplate my doom.

There are two ways it can go. Either I lose the contest and my life is over, or I win the contest and pay Mom for the Visa bill and my life is *still* over because they will never trust me again. Because Bridgette is perfect and Mal is Mal, and I will always be a disappointment. I'm not going to be able to eat my way out of it, and eating is the only thing I'm any good at.

I hear my phone chirp. Probably HeyMan texting me to eat again. I ignore it. A few seconds later, it rings. I check the display; it's Derek.

"Hi," I say, infusing my voice with maximum apathy.

"Hey, David! How's it going?"

"Fine."

"Listen, I had an idea. I heard you kicked butt at the qualifier. I think you're a winner."

"I didn't exactly win," I say. "Egon Belt was ahead all the way; then he stopped."

"Yeah, Hoover told me. But that Belt guy is an old man. You're just coming into your prime! There's big money in eating contests, you know. And I'm not just talking about Pigorino's. I figure with the right management, you could really rake it in. I could make that happen for you. You know how much money Joey Chestnut makes?"

"No idea."

"That's why you need a manager. It's not just winning contests—there are endorsements, sponsorships, honorariums, all kinds of ways to monetize your skills!"

He's talking so fast I wouldn't know what he was saying even if I knew what he was talking about.

"I don't need any more gift cards, Derek."

"I'm not talking gift cards. I'm talking cash. You don't even have to pay me—I'll take it out of your earnings, starting with the Pigorino Bowl. Fifteen percent."

"Listen, Derek, I've got to go."

"Okay, but you think about it. We'll make a great team."

I hang up. There is no way I want Derek for a manager. I open the refrigerator. I still have a whole head of cabbage in the crisper. I peel off the wilted outside leaves, cut it into wedges, and start eating.

< 160 >

‹ 30 ›
WAFFLES

It is the month of eating; it is the month of Mal.

Heads of cabbage, loaves of bread, giant bowls of spaghetti, a ten-pound watermelon, and gallon after gallon of water, juice, milk, and soda—I am a mouth, a tube, a human garbage disposal.

Mal loves to watch me eat. I'm sure he would pin me to his Wall if he could.

I am teaching Mal to eat new things. It's all about understanding the Rules.

It was actually HeyMan who helped me figure out Mal's Rules. He came by a couple of days ago while Mal and I were eating lunch. I had made myself a sub out of a loaf of French bread piled with salami, cheese, lettuce, and onions. Mal was eating potato chips and Cheerios out of separate bowls. Mal does not mix his foods.

"Does he eat anything that's not brown?" HeyMan asked.

"He eats Cheerios, potato chips, Ritz crackers, and fish sticks," I said.

"All brown," HeyMan said. "Light brown. He never eats anything green?"

"No. He also eats pizza crust, but only if it doesn't have a hint of sauce. And he won't eat the burnt parts."

"What about cookies?"

"I've seen him eat plain sugar cookies. He won't eat cookies that have chocolate chips or nuts."

"So his food has to be light brown and, um, homogeneous."

"Homogeneous?"

"The same all the way through."

"What about the fish sticks?"

"That's the exception that proves the rule."

"That saying makes no sense. If there's an exception, then there's no rule."

"Exactly. What about spicy? Does he like pepper?"

"He's more into bland. He does like a little crunch. I think he likes the sound, only it can't be too loud. Tortilla chips are too noisy for him."

"So it has to be light brown, plain, and just a little crunchy. You know what I bet he'd like? Waffles."

HeyMan was right. After Dad got home that night, I

< 162 >

walked over to the store and bought a box of frozen waffles. The next morning I popped four in the toaster. I put one on a plate and set it next to Mal's Cheerios. Mal pretended not to notice. If he senses eyes on him, he will not try anything new. I turned my back and stood at the counter and ate the other three waffles. When I turned around, Mal's waffle was gone and Mal was smiling into his Cheerios.

Since then, Mal and I have been experimenting with different foods. So far I have discovered that he will not eat French toast, cereals other than Cheerios, or fried shrimp. But we have waffles on the menu now, and I call that progress.

When Mal was six, we tried sending him to school. Not a regular school—a special school for kids with developmental disorders. It was a complete disaster. Mal wouldn't stop screaming.

Ever since then, we've been homeschooling him. A little over a year ago he learned to say "Okay." Since then, he hasn't learned much of anything. I know he's smart, but it's a different kind of smart. When he's in his room working on his Wall, it's clear that he is thinking complicated thoughts. But out in the real world his thoughts are overwhelmed by all the stuff coming at him in every direction.

Taking Mal for a walk outside is a major production. First, he has to wear his favorite black Iowa Hawkeyes hoodie, even if it's ninety degrees out. His shoes have to be tied just right—if they're too tight or too loose he won't go. He needs a handful of Cheerios in his pocket, and he needs his music. Mal likes music. Specifically, he likes this one song from the movie *Frozen*. I bet he's listened to it ten thousand times. After the first thousand times, Dad bought him a pair of headphones with an MP3 player built in so he can listen to it all he wants without driving the rest of us crazy.

I tie his shoes. I dig his Hawkeyes hoodie out of the laundry hamper. It's a little dirty, but Mal won't mind. I pour Cheerios in both his pockets. Mal puts on his headphones and turns on his song.

"You all set, buddy?"

"Okay!" he yells. Mal shouts when he's listening on his headphones.

We leave Arfie at home, because walking Arfie and Mal together is impossible. Arfie doesn't like being left behind, but he understands. We set out on our usual route, once around the block. There are many Things to examine. Mal collects a monarch wing, two willow leaves, and several dandelion blossoms. We discover a busy anthill and watch for a while. We do not step on any cracks. We eat some Cheerios. We meet Mrs. Rhodes walking her dachshund. Mal pets it on the head. Mal is good with dogs. Walking once around the block takes half an hour;

< 164 >

we are almost home when I sense a change in Mal. His steps become erratic, as if he has forgotten the rhythm of walking, his fists clench, and I can hear his breathing.

"We're almost home, buddy," I say. *Another hundred feet, Mal. Keep it together, dude!* "We'll be home in a minute. You can work on your Wall, okay?"

His jaw is tight and his breathing becomes louder as he strains the air in and out through clenched teeth.

"Almost there, Mal. We had a good walk, didn't we? Saw all those ants? Petted a doggie? Found some leaves? Come on, buddy. Arfie's waiting for us. We could have more waffles, right?"

Mal stops. He is rigid, fists at his sides, his entire body quivering with meltdown energy.

"Aw, crap, Mal. Do you have to?"

Mal screams.

I get behind him and clamp my arms around him.

Mal *howls.*

"Mal, it's okay. We're almost home."

And *shrieks* and *bucks* and *stomps* and kicks at my shins. We fall, landing on the Johnstons' lawn, me hanging on as tight as I can because I don't know what else to do. *This is a bad one,* I think, an instant before his head slams back into my chin. I almost let go, but I know I can't because if I do he's likely to run, and I don't think I can catch him if he does.

I roll onto my back, Mal on top of me, kicking and squirming and screaming. My head knocks Mal's headphones off. It takes a second for me to realize that there is no sound coming from them. No music. The battery must have died. That was what set him off.

I start singing. I'm not a good singer, but I've heard "Let It Go" from *Frozen* so many times I know it by heart, and I do my best. The first verse changes nothing—Mal is slamming his head back into my shoulder and kicking ferociously at my legs. Fortunately both his shoes have flown off. I keep singing, and as I sing and hold him, a part of me is thinking that it would be nice to be Mal.

Sure, he has his meltdowns, but only two or three a week, and they don't last long. He never seems to be bored, he always knows what he wants, and he has me and Mom and Dad to take care of him. Mal could have knocked my teeth out with that head butt, and nobody would have blamed him or tried to make him feel bad, because he is just Mal and although Mom still hopes he will start talking one day, we will always love him and accept him no matter what. Getting mad at Mal is like shouting at the moon.

In a way, Mal is invincible, immune, blameless. And here I am rolling around on the grass getting kicked in the shins and head-butted and singing a song I hate from a movie I hate, and I have my arms around my brother and

I won't let go because he is Mal, and I am me, and I am weirdly envious.

Halfway through the second verse, Mal stops shrieking and goes limp, as if somebody hit a switch. I keep singing. Mal is crying now, doing that sobbing, shaking thing that sometimes follows his meltdowns. I finish the song and start singing it again from the beginning.

"Okay," Mal says.

I let go slowly, ready to grab him if he goes berserk again. He seems to be okay. I look around and collect his shoes and the headphones. Stupid battery. Mrs. Johnston is looking out her window. On the street, a car is stopped, the driver staring at us. It's Al Chasen, a retired farmer who lives on the next block.

"You guys okay?" he asks.

"We're fine," I say. Tears are streaming down Mal's face. I rest my hand lightly on his shoulder. "Just a little meltdown."

Al nods, waves, and drives off. He knows about Mal. Everybody in Vacaville knows about Mal.

‹ 31 ›
WONTONS

That night Dad brings home takeout Chinese: General Tso's chicken and fried wontons. I make toaster waffles for Mal, and I tell Dad about his meltdown. Dad listens, nodding because he knows what it's like. We've been dealing with Mal meltdowns for years.

"That was smart," he says. "Singing to him."

"Thanks," I say. I don't often get told I'm smart.

Mal finishes his waffles and heads for the den, probably to watch *Frozen* for the umpteenth time. I open my fortune cookie.

> Opportunity eludes the timid mouse.

"I passed up an opportunity a few days ago," I say.

"Oh? What was that?"

"Derek offered to be my manager."

"Bridgette's Derek?"

"Yeah. He says there's a lot of money in professional eating."

"You told him no, I hope."

"I don't think I need a manager. Besides, he kind of bugs me."

Dad smiles. "He *can* be a bit irritating."

"Mal doesn't like him."

Dad nods. "Sometimes I think Mal knows more than he lets on. You know, David, we're very lucky. Mal is easy, compared to some kids in his situation. I have a friend at work—his thirteen-year-old son, Andrew, is autistic."

I'm surprised to hear him using the *A*-word, because usually we don't. Mom hates it. Even though she knows that Mal is autistic, even though she has shelves of books about autism, even though Mal's doctor has diagnosed him with autism, she won't use the word herself.

"In some ways Andrew is more developed than Mal. He can talk. But he can't be left alone for even five minutes."

"Why?"

"He hurts himself. He gets frustrated and bangs his head and hits things. It happens every day. Mal's episodes are mild by comparison."

"They sure don't feel mild when they're happening."

"I know."

"If he could just talk, he could tell us what's wrong. We could fix it."

"Like you fixed it this afternoon, by singing."

"I just made a lucky guess about what was bothering him."

"It was a good guess."

"Mom always talks about teaching Mal to do things, teaching him to act a certain way, teaching him what's okay, teaching him to use a spoon and how to tie his shoes . . . but it's really us learning about Mal, learning what works for him. We have to learn Mal's Rules."

"Mal's Rules." Dad nods slowly. "I like that."

"He sees things different."

"You're saying his autism is how he sees the world, and he's trying to teach *us*."

"Today he taught me to make sure his headphone battery is charged."

Dad laughs. "A good lesson," he says. "So how are *you*?"

How am I? The question takes me by surprise.

"I'm okay," I say. "Getting ready for the contest. Mal's helping me."

"How's he doing that?"

"He watches me practice. If I'm eating something

boring it's easier if I have an audience. Like, he watched me eat two heads of cabbage."

Dad manages not to frown. I can tell it takes some effort.

"You ate two heads of cabbage?"

"It's good for expanding stomach volume."

"David . . . I know this contest is important to you, but you have to be careful. When you talk about distorting your internal organs, I get concerned."

"It's temporary. I've read up on it."

"Online, I suppose."

"There's a lot of good information there. I'm not doing anything crazy like eating lightbulbs or scrap metal."

"But eating an entire head of cabbage . . ." He shakes his head and sighs. "Why couldn't you have just taken up basketball?"

"Why would I eat a basketball?"

"That's not what I meant."

"Eating is what I'm good at," I say.

He thinks about that for a moment. "You know what I used to be good at? Ollies."

"Ollies? You mean the skateboard trick?"

"Yeah. When I was in high school, I had the highest ollie in Des Moines. I could jump that board onto a picnic table."

He grins at my shocked expression. I never knew that Dad skateboarded, and ollies are *hard*. If you do it right, you can jump your board onto a curb—or something higher—and it looks as if the board is glued to your feet. I could never do one.

"My dream was to go pro," Dad says. "But I broke both my ankles doing a kickflip off the courthouse steps."

"So you quit?"

"Once my ankles healed I got back on my board, but I'd lost my edge. I was scared to attempt the more dangerous maneuvers. So I gave up my dream of becoming a skateboard hero and went to college instead." He grins and shrugs. "Anyway, I know how it feels when you're good at something. When you're the best, you just don't want to do anything else."

MORE CHEERIOS

The days pass. Mal and I get into a routine. Mal likes routines. We walk around the block every day, and there are no more battery fails and no more meltdowns. Mal is teaching me the finer points of Mal's Rules, which seem to be mostly about the finer points of boredom.

You think the card game War is monotonous? Mal is teaching me a card game he made up that takes boredom to a new level. The game is called "Okay." We take turns picking cards from a deck, and every time it's a face card we say, "Okay," and eat one Cheerio. We've been at it for half an hour, and I'm trying to sense whether he will have a fit if I stop playing.

I try to introduce a little variation by saying the actual name of the card. I turn up the jack of hearts and say, "Jack of hearts." Mal is okay with that. But when I turn up the king of diamonds and say, "Queen of spades," his lower lip comes out and the skin around his eyes gets tight, so I stop doing that. Clearly, one of Mal's Rules is that I call the cards by their correct names. I'm impressed that he knows them.

I get a reprieve when the doorbell rings. It's HeyMan. Or at least I think it's Hay. It's hard to tell with the felt hat and the giant wraparound sunglasses.

"Let me guess. Hollywood McDork."

"Close," HeyMan says. "Reginald Simon Mankowski."

"Secret identity?"

"Reginald was my grandpa. I was going through some of his stuff. He used to wear these glasses all the time for his cataracts. They fit over regular glasses—that's why they're so big." He tips his hat. "This was his hat. What do you think?"

"It's you."

"He had some cool ties, too. I'm thinking of reinventing myself. Back to the sixties."

"Has Cyn signed off on this?"

"I'm going over there later."

"Of course," I say, feeling resentful of his freedom. Some days I really hate being stuck at home.

Actually, I hate it all days.

"What's the matter?" HeyMan asks.

"Nothing."

"Okay," Mal says. He is still sitting on the carpet with his cards.

"Hey, Mal," HeyMan says. "How's it going?"

"Okay." Mal raises his head and looks at HeyMan. To my surprise, he looks straight at Hay's face without looking away.

"Playing cards, Mal?"

"New game." I explain the rules. "You want to play?"

"Uh, no thanks. I just wanted to run my new look past you."

"Mal had a bad meltdown last week." I don't know why I'm telling him this. I guess I just want him to know what I have to deal with. HeyMan has never witnessed a Mal meltdown, so he doesn't really get it.

"His headphones died," I say. "He freaked out right in front of the Johnstons'."

"Is he still listening to that same song?"

"Yeah. It's the only way he can deal."

"Needs his tunes. I get it."

No, you don't, I want to say.

"I don't think it's the music so much as the insulation."

HeyMan looks confused, so I explain.

"There's too much going on for him to process. He can't handle sudden noises, or noises from things he can't

< 175 >

see. It makes it so he can't think." I've never said that out loud before, but once I hear myself say it, it makes sense. The headphones aren't so much bringing him music, they're a filter between him and the noisiness of the outside world.

That gives me an idea. "Can I borrow those glasses?"

"What? No way! I just found them."

"I'll give them back. Come on."

"I wanted to show Cyn."

"She already knows you're a dork. Give me the glasses."

HeyMan backs away. "You're being weird. And Cyn doesn't think I'm a dork."

"Seriously, Hay. Just for today. I'll bring them back to you tonight."

He takes off the glasses. "What are you gonna do with them?"

"I'll tell you if it works."

After HeyMan leaves, I get Mal's Hawkeye hoodie out of the dryer and help him put it on. I take his headphones off the charger and tie his shoes on just right.

"Mal, I want us to try something new, okay?"

"Okay?" he says doubtfully.

I show him HeyMan's sunglasses. I put them on my face. "Pretty cool, huh?"

Mal is interested. He looks straight at me, right into my eyes. That gives me a shiver—Mal *never* looks anybody right in the eyes, but he can't see my eyes when I've got the glasses on, so it's okay. I take off the glasses; he looks away.

"You want to try them, buddy?"

Mal stares at the glasses.

"Come here. Let's look in the mirror." I guide him over to the full-length mirror by the front door. I see us standing together, me and my brother, and I realize how similar we are—same color hair, same nose, same chin, same eyebrows. But we are different, too. The way we hold our mouths, the way his shoulders are pulled in tight, the way I am looking straight at our reflection and he is staring off to the side. I put the glasses back on. His eyes shift. He is looking at me in the mirror now.

"You want to try them, Mal? Try on the glasses?"

"Okay." I can tell he is nervous. I take off the glasses. His eyes follow them. I put them in his hand. He turns them this way and that, examining them from every side, the way he would a new leaf. After about half a minute, he puts them on. They cover half his face.

He looks in the mirror, and he smiles.

‹ 33 ›

HALF-BAKED

Mal is transformed. With the enormous glasses and his headphones and his hoodie, he looks like a normal kid pretending to be a rap star. We step out the front door into the bright afternoon sunlight. He looks to the left, to the right, and up at the wispy white clouds.

Mal never does that. Mal is strictly ground oriented.

We walk down the front walkway, and I swear he has grown six inches. I've never seen Mal walk like this. We turn left at the sidewalk, and all the time his head is up, and he's looking around, and I am thinking that a miracle has occurred. We get to the end of the block. Mal turns left, our usual route.

"Mal," I say.

He stops. I point in the opposite direction.

"Want to do some exploring?"

Mal turns to face me.

"Try something new?" I say.

He doesn't move. I start across Elm Street, then look back to see if he's coming.

Mal steps off the curb. Together, we head into the unknown.

This can't be real, I think. But Mal seems fine. Better than fine. We are walking like two normal people. Two brothers taking a stroll up Elm Street. I imagine him talking:

Love my new glasses, big bro. How come you never thought of this before?

"I didn't get it, Mal. I thought you didn't look in my eyes because you didn't want to see them. I had it backwards, buddy."

Yeah, well, this is great. I can go anywhere.

"That's good, Mal. Now we can do all kinds of stuff." I'm talking out loud, just me, but it feels like a real conversation, even though he's not really talking and he probably can't hear me with "Let It Go" playing on his headphones.

I love being able to talk, David.

"It's nice, isn't it? You can tell us what you need."

That'll be nice. You guys just never seem to get it.

"I know, Mal. I'm sorry."

Like right now, I'm sort of hungry.

Uh-oh. I forgot to load up his pockets with Cheerios. I brace myself for a meltdown, but then notice that he is not digging in his pockets. His hands are swinging at his sides.

You know what would be great? Pizza.

Was that him or me?

I say, "You want to go get a pizza?"

"Okay," Mal says.

I can't believe we're doing this. It's nine long blocks to Pigorino's. I count them off, checking on Mal every few steps. He's doing fine. Can he do it? There are cars driving past us, a couple of barking dogs, the distant horn of a locomotive, unfamiliar buildings and trees and kids on bikes and a hundred other things with the potential to overwhelm him, but Mal remains invincible.

As we reach downtown the number of distractions doubles—people on the sidewalk, cars pulling in and out of parking spaces, a man dollying boxes off a truck, a woman mowing Vaccie's meadow. Mal stops to watch her. He points at the cow.

Vaccie.

"That's right, Mal. Vaccie. The big cow."

We're only a few steps from Pigorino's.

< 180 >

"Let's go inside, Mal. Let's get a pizza. You can have the crust."

Mal lets me guide him through the door. Vito, as usual, is manning the counter. He looks up.

"Hey, who's this? Is this your brother?"

"This is Mal," I say.

Mal is looking around at the tables, the flags on the walls, the turning fan overhead. It's the middle of the afternoon, so nobody's there. Mal is sniffing the air, working his nose like an excited dog.

"He a big eater too?" Vito asks.

"Mal's a specialist," I say. "He only eats certain things."

"I get that," Vito says. "I don't eat okra."

I order a pepperoni to go.

"Mal, it'll be a few minutes. Do you want to wait here, or go back outside and look at the cow?"

Mal doesn't move, so we sit down in one of the booths. Above the booth is a picture of the Colosseum in Rome. Mal stares up at the ancient building with the broken-off top.

"That's the oldest building in the world, Mal," I say. I have to almost yell to get through the music in his headphones. "It's almost as old as the pyramids." I'm not one hundred percent sure that's true, but it sure *looks* old.

Mal turns his attention to the red-pepper shaker.

"Careful with that, Mal. It's hot."

He puts it down, picks up the parmesan-cheese shaker, sniffs it, and puts it down, picks up the saltshaker and sprinkles some on the red-checked plastic tablecloth.

"Let's not make a mess, Mal."

"Okay." He pulls his arms off the table and starts to rock. It's not full-out rocking like he does sometimes, just a subtle back and forth. It's one of the things he does to calm himself.

"Just keep on rocking, Mal. Rock and roll. Stay *Frozen*; stay cool." Sometimes Mal's rocking indicates a coming meltdown, but not always. "Just keep listening to that song, buddy."

Vito, leaning over the counter, says, "Does he talk?"

"Not much. Is that pizza about ready?"

"Three minutes."

"I'll take it now."

"You want it half-baked?"

"Yeah. We're kind of in a hurry."

Two minutes later, Mal and I are back outside with our half-baked pizza. The woman is using a weed whacker to trim the grass around Vaccie's feet. Mal has to stop and stare at her. It seems to calm him. He likes steady, buzzing sorts of noises—things like trains and lawn mowers and big trucks on the highway. We watch for a few minutes, then head back toward home. The pizza smells great, even if it is underdone, so I open the box and grab a slice and eat it as we walk. Mal is watching me. It's kind of doughy, but not bad for only half cooked. I eat the saucy, cheesy, pepperoni part and offer Mal the crust. He accepts it solemnly and puts it in his pocket. By the time we get home, the pizza is gone except for the crusts in Mal's pockets.

Bridgette's car is parked in the driveway.

‹ 34 ›
Ice Cream and Pepper

Bridgette is sitting at the kitchen table eating chocolate-chip ice cream directly from the carton.

"Hey, Bridge," I say.

"Don't call me that." She doesn't bother to look up.

"Okay!" Mal shouts. He's still wearing his headphones.

"No classes today?" I ask.

She ignores us.

"Okay!" Mal gets even louder.

Bridgette closes her eyes and puts another spoonful of ice cream in her mouth.

"Mal wants you to look at him," I say.

Bridgette turns toward us as if it's the hardest thing

in the world. She sees Mal in his giant shades and head-phones, but hardly reacts. Both Mal and I are disap-pointed.

"We walked all the way downtown and back."

"So?" Her face looks puffy.

"No meltdowns. He's okay if he has the glasses on. It's like they're his superpower."

"Good for him." Her skin is red around her eyes and pale around her mouth.

"Did something happen?" I ask, trying to be nice.

"None of your business." If Bridgette were Mal, I'd say she was about to have a meltdown. She puts the top back on the ice-cream carton and pushes it aside. "I need Mom's number. I left my phone at school."

"We're only supposed to call her during the day if it's an emergency."

"Do you have her number or not?"

I take out my phone and read off Mom's number. She writes it down in her ever-present notebook.

"Have you been crying?" I ask, still trying to be nice.

She flashes her eyes at me. "Don't be stupid."

If that's the way she wants it, I can be nasty too.

"Did you get a C on a test or something?"

"That's *your* specialty."

"Did Derek break up with you?"

Score. Her eyes narrow. She starts to say something,

but I don't give her a chance. The words come spilling out of me.

"I figured he would, on account of you're way too *perfect* for him. All you think about is your stupid grades, and making everybody else look bad. You know, I do a lot around here." Her eyes are wet, but I can't stop myself. "I'm the one that figured out Mal needs headphones, and I'm the one who got him the sunglasses, and I spend time with him while you're off getting straight A's and being Little Miss Perfect—"

"Shut *up*." She's full-out crying now, but I don't stop.

"Now Mom is off doing something she's wanted to do forever but she's been stuck here because of Mal, and the only reason she can do it is because I'm taking care of Mal now and all you can think about is your problems and you don't care about anybody except yourself and your stupid boyfriend who doesn't really like you and—"

I'm interrupted by the blast of a horn. It sounds like it's right in front of the house.

Bridgette is looking past me.

"Where's Mal?" she says.

The front door is standing open. I run outside and see Mal and Arfie standing in the middle of the street, facing down a yellow pickup truck.

The red-faced, bearded guy driving the truck leans on

< 186 >

his horn again. Arfie barks, then runs back to the house. Mal is not moving.

"Mal!" I shout. He can't hear me with his headphones on.

The guy in the truck leans out his window. "Get off the street, numbnuts!"

Mal is frozen in place. I run out and grab his arm and pull. It's like trying to move a fireplug. Bridgette takes his other arm, and we drag him to the curb.

"You should lock him up," the truck guy says. I recognize him now. It's Jordan Pfleuger. He went to school with Bridgette. He still lives a few blocks away with his parents. Jordan has always been kind of a jerk.

"Sorry," I say.

"Sorry don't cut it, kid. You let that half-wit run loose, somebody's gonna get killed."

"Don't call him that," I say, walking toward the pickup.

"What? Half-wit? He is, ain't he?"

"The only *half-wit* here is *you*." I kick the truck as hard as I can. Jordan's eyes widen. He shoulders open the door, gets out, and looks at the dent.

"Why, you little . . ." He starts toward me with his fists clenched. I know I'm about to get my face smashed in, but I don't care. He's about to hit me when Bridgette steps between us and sticks something in his face. I hear a hiss, and Jordan screams. He drops to his knees and clamps his hands over his eyes.

"You blinded me!" he wails. "I'm blind!"

Bridgette is standing over him holding a small spray can.

"Oh shut up, Jordan," she says. "It's just a little pepper spray. You'll be fine." She looks at me and grins. "I've been wanting to do that since high school."

We get Mal back inside. He's not having a meltdown—it's the opposite. Sometimes when he gets really tired, he can hardly walk or keep his eyes open, and between our trip to Pigorino's and the pickup-truck incident, he's had a full day. We help him upstairs to his room. He curls up on his bed. I take off his headphones and glasses and pull the bedspread over him. He is asleep within seconds. He'll probably sleep for hours.

Bridgette and I go back downstairs. We don't talk about our argument. She puts away the ice cream and grabs her car keys and starts to leave.

"Aren't you going to call Mom?" I ask.

She shakes her head. "I'll talk to her later."

I follow her to the front door. Jordan and his yellow pickup are gone. I guess he wasn't blinded after all.

"I'm sorry about Derek," I say.

She nods. "We'll work it out."

< 188 >

"So you're not actually broken up?"

"He's just being a jerk."

"You can always pepper-spray him."

She shoots me a quick look, sees I'm kidding, and smiles faintly.

"Thanks for taking care of Mal," she says.

< 189 >

‹ 35 ›

PIZZA BIANCA

"You can't have your glasses back," I tell HeyMan. "Mal needs them."

"What? No way!"

"They're cheap plastic glasses. I looked them up online. They sell for fifteen bucks new."

"Oh. Okay, I'll sell them to you for twenty."

I hear laughter in the background.

"Is that Cyn? Let me talk to her."

A second later, Cyn is on the phone.

"Mal has become attached to Hay's sunglasses," I say. "Tell him to give them to him."

I hear Cyn tell HeyMan to let Mal keep the glasses.

"They're family heirlooms!" he whines.

"David says Mal needs them," Cyn says. I hear

muttering, then HeyMan's assent. Lately, he will do anything she asks.

"Thanks," I say. "So what are you guys up to?"

"Going to the Cineplex in Indianola. HeyMan wants to see something with cars blowing up. Want to come?"

I consider it for a moment, but lately it feels weird hanging with HeyMan and Cyn, the three of us, like I'm an extra in their little movie.

"I think I'll just chill. Dad just got home with a bucket of chicken from Casey's. I'm thinking if Mal wears the magic glasses he might actually eat some."

"Good luck with that."

"It's worth a try."

Mal won't eat the chicken with or without the glasses, so I make him a waffle. I tell Dad about the long walk we took. Dad is impressed. I don't mention Jordan and his pickup truck.

"It makes sense," he says. "Mal has difficulty processing sensory input. The glasses give him a visual buffer zone. We should've thought of it before."

"Maybe we could make him a buffer suit," I suggest. "Like a special suit with headphones and dark glasses and cushions everywhere. Like the Michelin Man. He'd be invulnerable."

Dad laughs.

Mal says, "Okay."

Dad regards him thoughtfully. "Sometimes, Mal, I think you understand every word we say."

Mal looks straight at him through his sunglasses and smiles.

I don't think Mal understands most of what we say, but it's fun to think that maybe he might. I've tested him by saying nonsensical things.

"Mal, *arg ung dribblewacky, strug twiller nougat?*"

"Okay," Mal will say.

"*Ribbolito! Sanger dorf.*"

"Okay," Mal will agree.

But he does understand when he is being talked to, and he knows the difference between a question and a command, and he knows the names of playing cards. He likes questions. He does not like commands.

The next day we go on another adventure. The same adventure, actually. We walk downtown to Pigorino's. It goes like before, except there is nobody mowing Vaccie's little meadow. Mal stops and stares at Vaccie for more than a minute, as if willing the woman to reappear with her weed whacker.

He seems more comfortable inside Pigorino's. He's been there before, so we are on familiar ground. Vito is in a good mood, so I decide to pump him for information about the upcoming contest.

"So, Vito," I say, "you gonna be making BLDs for the big contest?"

"If Papa wants BLDs, I'll make BLDs."

"Is that the plan?" I'm hoping it isn't. If I have to start practicing on BLDs it'll cost me forty bucks a pie.

Vito shrugs. "Papa does what Papa wants to do. Only thing I know is it's gonna be crazy. We got twenty-four eaters qualified for the big event. That's a lot of BLDs, and they aren't easy, especially since we'll be working out of our concession on the fairgrounds. We'd need to add a flat-top for the eggs and hash browns. It'll be tough enough just setting up extra ovens—those things weigh about eleven hundred pounds each, and we'll need two. We got a crew at the fairgrounds now adding a wing to the concession. This contest is costing Papa a fortune."

That's the most words I've ever heard come out of Vito's mouth.

"Most contests, like the Famiglia one, are just cheese pizzas," I tell him. "That way, more slices get eaten. You should ask Papa if he'd rather see a headline reading 'Local Teen Devours Fifty Slices of Pigorino's Pizza' or 'Teen Almost Finishes One Pizza.'"

"You really think you could eat fifty slices?"

"Joey Chestnut ate forty-five."

"You're no Joey Chestnut."

"People keep telling me that."

"How many pizzas you think we'll need?"

"If you make plain cheese pizzas . . . twenty-four eaters . . . maybe seventy-five or eighty?"

"Eighty? How do you figure? Everybody's not gonna eat like you."

"Well, a lot of it won't get eaten. You cut a pizza into eight slices, and if a guy eats just nine slices, you still have to have two pizzas for him, right? And most of the eaters will eat at least that much. Me and Egon Belt will probably need five or six each."

Vito nods. "You make a good point." He leans on the counter and thinks for a moment. "Those BLDs take almost half an hour to bake. Plain cheese, I can get those in and out in five minutes, plus we can fit more in the oven. Eighty cheese would be easier than twenty-four BLDs. Cheaper, too. Papa would like that." He stands up straight. "I'll talk to him. So, what can I get you?"

"A sausage-and-mushroom. And I was wondering if you could make a kid-size plain for Mal."

"Plain cheese?"

"No. Just the crust. No sauce, no cheese, no nothing." I look over at Mal, who is sitting at the table moving the condiments around the checkered vinyl tablecloth like pieces on a chessboard.

"Seriously? Okay, one Pizza Bianca, naked."

"Pizza Bianca? It has a name?"

"Yeah, but nobody's ever ordered one before."

"Mal is very unusual."

< 195 >

< **36** >

SOGGY CRUST

The Pizza Bianca is a huge hit with Mal. Every day around lunchtime, with no prompting from me, he puts on his gear and stands waiting by the front door. I try to introduce a small variation every time, changing our route, or walking faster or slower, trying and failing to teach Mal to skip. One time I ask Vito to put a single disk of pepperoni in the middle. Mal is not bothered by that. He eats the outside, then offers me the part he doesn't want, a perfectly round micro pizza, carefully nibbled to within a quarter inch of the pepperoni disk.

"Thank you, Mal," I say. Since he seems so comfortable at Pigorino's, we are eating our pizzas there instead of getting takeout. There is one particular booth Mal likes—the one with the picture of the Colosseum.

I've been working on my technique. I have the soft part

of the pizza nailed: reverse fold, bite-bite-bite, and what I call the infinite gulp. Learning to swallow while biting is the key. Normal eaters chew, then swallow, then chew. But I have trained myself to swallow continuously while chewing. The crust is the hardest part, and I mean that in both senses. The water-dunk is essential. I come up with a system where I leave the first crust in my glass of water and let it sit while I eat the soft part of the next slice. That extra few seconds of soaking softens it just enough that I can save a few seconds when I eat it. Waterlogged pizza crust is not the most wonderful thing I've ever eaten, but it goes down a lot faster. Like I say, it's all about technique.

That daily pizza is my speed training. For capacity, I've been eating heads of cabbage and drinking lots of water. My stomach is getting noticeably bigger, not so much in the way it looks from the outside but in how much it can hold.

The days go by quickly now that Mal and I have our routine down. I don't see much of HeyMan and Cyn— they're always doing something. They always invite me to join them, but I have Mal most of the time.

HeyMan texts me a couple times a day, and we talk on the phone, but I'm getting irritated with him. He keeps talking about this new Xbox package he wants to buy with "his money" from the contest. He's already guilting me in case I don't win.

"I got the Xbox on hold," he says. "So I'll have it the day after the contest, unless you choke."

"I might not win," I tell him. "But I won't choke."

"Yeah, whatever, but you know we're counting on you, me and Cyn."

I don't need to hear that kind of stuff. I talk to Cyn sometimes too, and that's not as bad except she always wants to know how I'm feeling, and I can't tell if she's asking because she cares or because of her investment. Either way, it makes me squirm.

Mostly I spend my evenings in front of the TV or rereading Walking Dead comics or watching eating contests on YouTube.

Mom will be home Friday evening. It feels like she just left, but I'll be glad to have her back. I think about how happy she'll be about Mal now that he has his magic glasses and she can take him places she never could before. Last week, Dad took Mal to the hardware store. He loved it. While Dad was chatting with Mr. Hanks, Mal fell in love with the nuts-and-bolts section. He particularly liked the stainless-steel hex bolts, so Dad bought him an assortment in different sizes. The last few days, he's been spending more time screwing nuts on and off those bolts than he has on his Wall. I bet Mom could even take him to her yoga. Just give him some bolts and he'd keep himself busy for an hour.

< 198 >

I've been managing not to think too much about the Visa bill. Every time I walk past the bureau in the front hall I think about that envelope and I get a little queasy. I shove it to the back of my mind. First I have to win the contest; then I can deal with it.

Friday morning, the day before the contest, I eat two heads of cabbage for breakfast. My speed training has been going well—I'm down to fourteen seconds per slice. I'm all set for transportation. Vacaville doesn't have regular bus service, but there's a special 4-H bus leaving at seven in the morning for all the farm kids, and they said Cyn and Hay and I could ride along.

I'm ready.

< 199 >

‹ 37 ›

SALMON

Dad gets home early, right after lunch, and we launch into a major housecleaning. It's a big job—the house is kind of messy—but after a couple of hours we have it looking more or less the way it did before Mom left. Even Mal is helping, lining up his nuts and bolts on the coffee table, rearranging a few items on his Wall, and for the first time ever, attempting to make his bed. He gets the spread on sideways, but it's a good effort.

Once the house is straightened up, the three of us make an expedition to the grocery store. Mom will be home around six, and we want to welcome her with a nice dinner. We buy a side of salmon for the grill, salad greens, a loaf of French bread, and three boxes of frozen toaster waffles. Mal is on his best behavior. He is fascinated by the rows of potato-chip bags and insists on carrying a bag of ripple chips. In the produce section, still hugging his bag of chips, he examines the fruits and vegetables. He stops in front of some knotty, bulbous green vegetables.

"That's kohlrabi, Mal," Dad says. "Do you want some?"

Mal moves on to the stalks of Brussels sprouts.

"I don't think he'd like kohlrabi," I say. "It's green."

Dad laughs. "I don't think anybody likes kohlrabi."

"Then why do they sell it?"

"It's one of life's mysteries."

When we get home Bridgette is there, finding things to clean that Dad and I overlooked.

"You guys are hopeless," she says as she dusts the top of the refrigerator, but she's smiling.

It's a good feeling, the four of us working together, getting ready for Mom. In my whole life I've never gone this long without seeing her. I'm feeling happy and excited and proud when her car pulls into the driveway. We all run out to help with her luggage. She's brought presents for all of us: a book with pictures of all kinds of tree leaves for Mal, a University of Minnesota sweatshirt for Dad, a box of colored felt-tip pens for Bridgette, and for me, a T-shirt with the entire front printed like a pepperoni pizza. I put it on right away. I look like I have a terminal case of gigantic measles, but I love it.

"Very stylish," Mom says. "I thought you could wear it for your big day tomorrow."

"It's perfect," I say. *Everything* is perfect. Dad is whistling as he gets the grill ready for the salmon; Bridgette is happily cleaning, Mal is paging through his new leaf book, and I am telling Mom about Mal's new superpowers as she pours herself a glass of wine. The good feelings last through dinner, even though the salmon is a little undercooked and Mal drops a waffle on the floor for Arfie. Mom doesn't get even a little upset at that—she laughs like it's the funniest thing ever.

"We had one boy at language camp, Valdis, who insisted on sharing his lunch with the squirrels. He was from Latvia. He could speak only Russian and Klingon."

"Klingon?" I say.

"Apparently they have *Star Trek* in Latvia. Valdis was a smart kid. By the time he left, he could speak enough English to translate all his Klingon phrases." She eats a piece of nearly raw salmon. "This is so good! I really missed you guys. And Mal, so grown-up now!" She touches his shoulder. "Going to the grocery store! I'm proud of you."

Mal chews intently on a bite of waffle.

"The sunglasses help," I say, begging for a little credit.

"That was brilliant, David." She turns to Bridgette. "And you—a perfect score on your chemistry exam! That's wonderful! I should go away more often."

"Please don't," Dad says with a grin. "We're helpless without you."

After dinner, Bridgette and I clean the kitchen. Dad and Mal are in the backyard. Mom is on her computer, catching up with her e-mail and so forth. I ask Bridgette about Derek. She stiffens, then shrugs.

"We went out last night," she says.

"No pepper-spray events?"

She laughs. "No pepper spray."

"So you're back together?"

"It's complicated."

I'm not sure I want to hear about complications.

"How's *your* girlfriend?" she asks, shifting the subject.

"*My* girlfriend?"

"Cyn. Isn't that her name?"

"Cyn's not my girlfriend. She's just a friend." I'm surprised Bridgette doesn't know that. But at least she's trying—usually she couldn't care less about what's going on in my life. "Actually, I think she might be HeyMan's girlfriend. It's complicated."

Bridgette bumps me with her hip and smiles.

"It always is."

Our heart-to-heart brother-sister conversation is interrupted by a screech from the next room. It's not Mal this time. It's Mom.

‹ 38 ›
SLIDER

Mom is sitting at her laptop with a horrified expression on her face.

"What's wrong?" Bridgette asks.

Mom looks up at us.

"My credit card's been hacked. Two thousand dollars!" Mom points at the display.

Dad comes in and looks over her shoulder at the statement displayed on her computer.

"V. B. Schutlebecker. Who is V. B. Schutlebecker?" he asks.

"I have no idea! But I'm sure I didn't buy *anything* from *anybody* for that much money. And they say my account is past due! How can that be? I always pay right away."

"It says it was due weeks ago," Dad says.

"Yes, but I'm certain I didn't get a bill. Two thousand dollars! And they want a late fee, and interest!"

"You've looked through all the mail?"

"As soon as I got home!"

"V. B. Schutlebecker Enterprises," he reads. "Could be anything. You'd better get on the phone and report it. If somebody stole your card number, you're not responsible. But you have to let them know right away."

"I'll call them right now."

I am standing in the doorway, my entire life crumbling inside me. If she calls the credit-card company, they'll be able to trace the sale. Virgil Schutlebecker, aka the Gurge, will prove that he sold the hot dog on BuyBuy and shipped it to me. There is no way I can wriggle out of it . . . and I'm not sure I want to. The guilt of what I did has been eating away at me, and I don't think I can stand it for another second.

"Mom," I say.

"Just a minute, David. I need to take care of this right now."

"Mom!"

She puts down the phone and looks at me. I take a deep breath. My hands are shaking, and the top of my head wants to float away. My voice comes out high-pitched and alien-sounding.

"I know who stole your credit-card number."

< 205 >

With a shaky voice and sweating palms, I tell them what happened. They listen in total shock, especially my mom, who is looking at me as if I've turned into a pile of dog dung.

"It was an accident," I say.

"An accident?" Dad's not exactly shouting, but he's talking incredibly loud. "It was an accident you took your mother's credit-card information and used it to make a purchase?"

"Not that part," I admit. "But it was only supposed to be for twenty dollars."

Mom says, "David . . ." She is unable to continue. She looks as miserable as I feel.

Dad is pacing back and forth, breathing loudly through his nose.

"Two thousand dollars," he says through clenched teeth. "Even if it was twenty cents, the fact remains that you *stole* money from your mother. For a hot dog! *A hot dog?*"

"A *half* hot dog."

"That is not relevant! What were you thinking?"

Why do parents always ask that?

"I don't know," I say.

"You don't *know*? Is that your excuse?"

"Look, I'm sorry. I'm just telling you what happened."

Bridgette is sitting on the side chair, judging me with her eyes.

"If you needed money, you could have asked," Mom says in her pretending-to-be-calm voice.

"You weren't here," I say. It's not true, but I don't care. "I was home taking care of Mal, like I always do."

"That is not relevant!" Dad says again.

"I'm sorry! What else do you want me to say? I screwed up."

"You certainly did. And you can forget about that contest tomorrow. You can forget about leaving this house for the next . . . forever."

"The contest is so I can pay you back," I say. "That's the whole point."

"That is *not* the whole point. The money's not the point. The point is that you've betrayed our trust in you."

"Trust?" Now I'm yelling. "You hardly pay any attention to me. I'm just here to babysit Mal, and you know it. All you care about is Mal, and Bridgette's stupid grades, and"—I look at Mom—"your stupid language camp. And all *you*"—I look at Dad—"all *you* do is go to work and come home and everybody's supposed to be so proud of you, but none of us know what it is you actually *do* all day. Meanwhile I'm just this *thing* that happened to show up between Bridgette and Mal."

They are all gaping at me. Even Bridgette is sitting with her usually prim lips hanging open.

Dad says in a slightly calmer voice, "David, that is simply not true. And this is not about us, it's about your behavior."

"My behavior is the same as always. I made one mistake. One! Mal can have his meltdowns and break stuff and eat potato chips all day long and you go, 'Oh, well, that's just Mal.' But I do one stupid thing in my entire life and I try to fix it on my own, and all of a sudden I'm a piece of crap. It's not fair. It's NEVER fair. I don't—"

A piercing shriek echoes through the house, like the siren that goes off before the end of the world.

Mom says, "Where's Mal?"

‹ 39 ›
VANILLA

It's a bad one.

Mal is in the backyard, banging his head on the fence.
Dad tries to grab him, but Mal flails, arms and feet flying.
Dad catches an elbow in the face, and his nose gushes
blood. Mal is screaming so loud it hurts my ears, and
his eyes are rolled up in his head so far all I can see is
white. Mom comes running out with the rug. Mal kicks it
away, then kicks me in the shin so hard I collapse in pain.
Dad grabs him from behind and wraps his arms around
Mal's, and they fall to the grass, Mal on top. Mal slams
his head back and hits Dad on the mouth, all the while
kicking furiously. Mom is standing by helplessly with the
rug while Bridgette, phone in hand, is yelling "Should I

call nine-one-one?" I manage to grab Mal's feet and hold them. Mal's screams have gotten hoarse, as if his throat has shredded itself.

I hear Mr. Johnston's voice from the other side of the fence. "Everything okay over there?"

"We're fine," I yell back, even though it's light-years from the truth. I run back into the house for Mal's headphones and sunglasses. When I get back outside, Mal's screams have become a piteous, sobbing wail—it's harder to listen to than the screams.

Suddenly Dad shouts in pain. Mal has sunk his teeth into his wrist. Dad yanks his arm free, and Mal gets loose; he's on his feet running toward Bridgette. She yelps and drops her phone, spreading her arms out to catch him. Mal veers right and heads for the other side of the yard. He runs straight into the privacy fence. He hits it so hard, I half expect him to keep going, leaving a kid-shaped hole behind.

The fence holds. Mal bounces off it and lands on his back. Dad and I are running over to him, me with the headphones and glasses, Mom right behind us with the rug. But Mal doesn't stay down. He jumps up and runs along the fence in a complete panic. I drop the headphones and glasses and cut him off at the back gate, hitting him like a tackle taking down a wide receiver. Mal hits the ground hard, and a second later I hear the labored *squee, squee* of him straining for breath.

"Breathe, Mal," I hear myself say. "Breathe."

Dad is there, and Mom with the rug. She spreads it on the grass.

Squee, squee . . .

Dad lifts Mal under the arms and pulls him over the rug while I go for the headphones.

Squee . . . Mal gasps and takes a full, shuddering breath. Mom pulls the short end of the rug over him while I clamp his headphones on him and turn on "Let It Go."

"Should we roll him up?" Dad asks.

"Wait a minute," I say. Mal's forehead has a nasty scrape from when he hit the fence. His eyes are squeezed shut, his arms are rigid at his sides, and he's breathing hard. I put my hands on his shoulders. "It's okay, Mal," I say. "It's okay."

"Okay," he says.

"Do you want to be a burrito?"

He opens his eyes and looks straight up at the deep-blue evening sky.

"Okay."

Gently, we roll him up in the rug. I find his sunglasses where I dropped them and put them on his face. Mal turns his head this way and that, looking at each of our faces, all of us kneeling around him as if he's a miracle child in a manger. Arfie, who has been observing all this human drama from safely beneath the picnic table, ambles over and licks Mal's face.

Mal smiles. His smile seems to radiate peace onto all of us, and for a moment I think that everything will be like it was at dinner, when nobody was mad at anybody and we were all happy together. And for a few seconds, it's true.

Mom says, "Honey, let's get you cleaned up." She is talking to Dad, who is bleeding from his nose, his lip, and his wrist.

Dad nods. "David, will you stay with him? You too, Bridgette."

"Okay," Mal mutters sleepily. He is slipping into post-meltdown lethargy. Bridgette and I sit there without talking for what seems like a long time. I keep waiting for her to berate me for the Visa-bill thing, but she doesn't. She just sits quietly on the lawn with me and Mal and Arfie. The sun is setting. The mosquitoes will be out soon. I hear our neighbor's back door slam—Mr. Johnston has probably been watching through a crack in the fence: *The Crazy Millers Show* is much better than whatever's on TV.

After a while, Bridgette says, "You know how I said it's complicated? With Derek?"

"Yeah?"

< 212 >

"It's not. Actually, I broke up with him."

"Good."

"All he cares about is himself. And he has no sense of humor. At all."

"You just figured that out?"

She gives me a sharp look.

"I never liked him much," I say.

"Well, I did. Or at least I thought I did. But I think mostly the reason we stayed together as long as we did was because I hate being alone. You've got your friends, and you know everybody in town, and you have Mom and Dad and Mal. But I didn't know anybody at Simpson, so when I started seeing Derek I sort of latched on, you know?"

"Maybe now you can latch on to somebody with a sense of humor."

Bridgette smiles and looks down at Mal.

"I think first I have to figure out how to latch on to myself."

Mom comes back outside. "How is he?"

"Sleeping."

"Do you think we can unwrap him and carry him to his room? I want to take a look at that cut on his head."

I ask Mal if he's ready to be unburritoed, but he's too deep in sleep to hear me. We unroll him slowly; then Mom picks him up in her arms like a baby. Mal weighs almost seventy pounds, but she lifts him easily. We take him upstairs and lay him on his bed. Mom gets her first-aid kit and cleans the scrape on his forehead. She smears on some ointment and puts a Band-Aid on it.

"Can you sit with him a while?" she asks me.

"I'll stay with him," Bridgette says.

Mom and I look at each other, surprised. I don't think we realized until that moment how rare it was for Bridgette to spend time alone with Mal. She had always been so busy with school and her many extracurricular activities that Mal duty had always fallen to the rest of us.

"I'll read to him," Bridgette says. Mom likes us to read to Mal, even when he is sleeping. It doesn't matter what it's about; the point is to fill his ears with the sound of words. Bridgette picks a book from the shelf next to Mal's bed, a picture book about a dog, one of Mal's favorites. As we leave the room she opens the book and begins to read. "Five little puppies dug a hole under the fence . . ."

While Bridgette sits with Mal, I finish cleaning the kitchen. Mom and Dad are in their bedroom. The barely audible buzz of them talking is making my ears itch, because I know they're talking about me, about what a thieving, lying wretch I've turned out to be. I wipe down the counters extra carefully. I may be a thieving, lying wretch, but

< 214 >

at least they can't accuse me of not performing this simple household chore.

When I've finished cleaning, I find a half-empty carton of vanilla Häagen-Dazs in the freezer. I stand at the sink and eat it slowly, letting the silky-smooth ice cream soothe me from the inside out. When I'm done I throw the carton in the trash. I leave the dirty spoon in the sink because I am not, after all, perfect.

‹ 40 ›
ONION RINGS

Sleep? Not hardly.

I lie in bed with the lights out, listening to the sounds of my wounded family: the murmur of Bridgette reading to Mal, who is almost certainly asleep, and the fainter buzz of Mom and Dad in their bedroom downstairs, still talking. I wish I knew what they were saying, but then I'm glad I can't. It's bad enough that I can imagine it.

What on earth are we going to do with David?

Send him to military school, I guess. Clearly, he can't be trusted.

Maybe we should send Mal away, too. Have him locked up in an asylum.

We could lock them both up in institutions. That would solve everything.

My thoughts shift to tomorrow. My whole life for the past several weeks has been about getting ready for the Pigorino Bowl, and they won't let me go. As guilty as I feel, that seems horribly unfair. I think about getting up in the morning and going down to breakfast and facing them, the looks in their eyes, the set of my father's jaw, the cut on his lip, the look of betrayal and disappointment on Mom's face.

Around midnight, I hear Bridgette closing Mal's door softly, tiptoeing down the stairs. The sound of her car door shutting, the burble of the engine, the sound of tires on asphalt as she backs out of the driveway. I hear Mom and Dad talking again. How do they find so much to say?

Their low voices fade; I now hear only the rustling of leaves outside my window and the buzz of the refrigerator, and I remember something that happened a long time ago.

I was about Mal's age. Dad was taking me to a Triple-A Baseball game in Des Moines—the Iowa Cubs versus the Memphis Redbirds. I'd never been to a ball game before, and this was a whole day with my dad, hot dogs, baseball, the big city—I was beyond excited. We were halfway there when he got a call on his phone. He talked for a few minutes to some guy named Frank; then he hung up and sighed.

"Change of plans, David. I'm sorry."

Instead of going to Principal Park, we drove to a big warehouse in West Des Moines where we picked up a refrigerator part in a long cardboard box. From there, we headed back into the city.

"One of my clients, PackMor, has an emergency situation," Dad explained. "One of their cooling units broke down, and they've got six thousand pounds of beef about to go bad. I need to get this part over to them pronto."

"I thought you just sold stuff," I said. "How come you have to deliver it, too?"

"Well, we have a little problem with our drivers, David. They won't cross the picket line."

"What's a picket line?"

Dad explained that the meat-packers were on strike because they weren't being paid enough. The truck drivers, in support of the meat-packers, were refusing to make deliveries to PackMor.

"The meat-packers have a point," Dad said. "PackMor has been stonewalling them for years, and they've finally had enough. But I have my job to consider, and PackMor is one of my biggest customers. Don't worry; we'll still be able to catch the last few innings."

PackMor was a huge collection of cinder-block and steel-sided buildings surrounded by a chain-link fence. Several dozen men and women carrying signs were clustered near the front. As we pulled up to the gate, the protestors waved signs at us saying things like ON STRIKE, and UNFAIR!, and HONEST WORK DEMANDS HONEST PAY. Some of them were shouting at us. One guy banged his sign on the hood of our car; another guy pulled him away. Dad kept his eyes straight ahead the whole time. A man came out of the building and opened the gate. We drove through. We took the refrigerator part inside and Dad installed it. It only took about twenty minutes. I hadn't even known he could do that kind of work.

"I was a repair technician before I got into sales," he told me.

"Those people with the signs, they all work here?"

"Some of them are from the union." He looked around to make sure nobody was listening. "The strikers are good people. I feel terrible about crossing their picket line."

"Then why do it?"

He sighed. "David . . . this company is like a lot of other companies. It's run by people who are sometimes selfish and greedy. They think they have to be that way to make a profit, and if they don't make a profit, they don't stay in business and those strikers don't have a job. But sometimes the owners get a little too selfish and greedy—I think that's what happened here."

"So you think the strikers are in the right?"

"Essentially, yes. But if I hadn't brought this part through the picket line, there would have been a lot of wasted meat, and the company would have taken a big loss. Not to mention I would have lost a client." He wiped grease off his hands with a rag. "Sometimes you just have to do the wrong thing for the right reason."

We made it to the ballpark in time for the sixth inning. I ate three trays of onion rings. The Iowa Cubs lost.

It's one o'clock in the morning, and I'm still not sleepy. I turn on the light and send a couple of quick texts to HeyMan and Cyn, then fire up my laptop and start typing.

> Dear Mom and Dad,
>
> First thing is I'm sorry for everything. I know I messed up. And you're probably going to get even madder because I'm on my way to Des Moines for the contest. I'm sorry.
>
> I'm sorry for yelling at you and making Mal have a meltdown and I'm really sorry he bit you, Dad. I'm sorry about the $2,000. I know it's not about the money, but the only way I know to pay you back is to win the Pigorino Bowl.
>
> Mal wants me to go. I've been practicing with him all month and he gets that what I'm doing is important and I've taught him to eat two new things since you left, Mom. He can go places now

without freaking, and I think he really is going to talk any day now, just like you want.

So I'm going to the contest and after I get back you can lock me in my room or just never talk to me again but no matter if I win or not I will pay you back and I promise I will never do anything like this again for the rest of my life even if I spend it in a dungeon.

Love,
David

I sleep a little bit after that, but I'm awake by the time the first glimmer of light appears in the sky. I put on my pizza T-shirt and sneak downstairs. I leave the letter on the kitchen table, let myself out, and head over to HeyMan's.

< 221 >

‹ 41 ›

KRAUT AND BEER

The 4-H bus is insane. Cyn and Hay and I are crammed into one seat at the very back, with me in the corner. The rest of the bus is jam-packed with farm kids from Vacaville, Halibut, and Blue Prairie. Nearly all of them have brought lunch boxes with them, and half of them are already eating. The air is thick with the smell of salami and sauerkraut. Jooky Garafalo holds the world record for sauerkraut—six pounds in twelve minutes. He can keep that record, as far as I'm concerned.

Most of the kids know each other from 4-H meetings. Everybody is talking and yelling and laughing and munching at the same time. Halfway there, somebody starts singing "Ninety-Nine Bottles of Beer." To my surprise, Cyn joins in, then HeyMan starts singing too. I put my hands over my ears and scrunch down in the seat. I have to stay focused.

. . . Ninety-six bottles of beer on the wall,
ninety-six bottles of beer.
If one of those bottles should happen to fall,
ninety-five bottles of beer on the wall.
Ninety-five bottles of beer . . .

I try to block out the noise and the sauerkraut smell and the guilt I'm feeling for disobeying my parents. I imagine myself eating pizza, a torrent of crust and sauce and cheese flowing into my mouth and down my throat. I think of what Derek told me: *You are a tube. A three-hole donut.* I take a breath through my mouth, my lungs fill with sauerkraut-infused oxygen. A wave of nausea passes over me. I groan.

"Are you okay?" Cyn asks.

"How much farther?" I ask.

"Probably another fifty verses."

"Who eats sauerkraut for breakfast?"

"That would be Will Meyer. I think he's doing it to be funny."

"I am not amused."

. . . Eighty-nine bottles of beer on the wall,
eighty-nine bottles of beer. . . .

Cyn resumes singing. By the time they get to sixty-five bottles of beer on the wall the sauerkraut smell is mostly gone. Either that or I'm used to it. It's still a long ride. By the time the bus pulls up to the fairgrounds' main gate only six bottles of beer remain on the wall.

The Iowa State Fair is one of the biggest in the country. They get a million visitors a year—people come from all over the state to gawk at the biggest hog. They watch the tractor-pull, the outhouse-race, and the rubber-chicken-throwing contest. They come for the food: corn dogs, elephant ears, kettle corn, and an assortment of even stranger foods like Zombie Cones, chicken-fried bacon, and fried peanut butter and jelly on a stick. I am not kidding.

We pile off the bus and head for the admissions kiosk to buy tickets. HeyMan thinks I should pay for him and Cyn.

"We're your investors," he argues.

"So invest another twelve bucks. I've only got twenty left, and I haven't even bought anything yet."

"You're gonna be eating all that pizza. What do you need to buy?"

"Maybe one of those hats." I point at a guy wearing a tall yellow hat printed like a cob of corn.

"You wear that and somebody's liable to take a bite out of you."

"Whatever. You still have to buy your own tickets."

"Cheapskate."

We each buy our own ticket and push through the turnstiles into the fairgrounds.

"We have lots of time before the contest," Cyn says. "What are you guys going to do?"

"Eat," HeyMan says. "Are you hungry?"

"Not at the moment," Cyn says. She's looking at her phone. "I have a list. I want to see the fine-arts show, I want to check out the textile exhibit, and of course I have to see the chickens. The chickens are the best."

"Chickens sound good," HeyMan says. "Fried or baked?"

Cyn swats him on the arm.

"What else?" I ask her.

"The Butter Cow," she says.

Of course. The Butter Cow. I forgot about that. I'd been to the state fair several times, but not for the past few years. With Bridgette in school and Mal being Mal, taking David to the state fair wasn't high on my parents' priority list. But the few times we did go, we'd always gone to see the Butter Cow.

"Let's do the cow first," I say.

The Butter Cow is an almost full-size sculpture of a cow made of butter. It's located in the Agriculture Building in a refrigerated display case. It is spectacular.

A girl is passing out information pamphlets. I take one and learn that this particular butter cow stands five feet eight inches at the shoulder, weighs six hundred pounds, and contains enough butter for 20,000 slices of toast.

"What do you suppose they do with all the butter after the fair?" I ask.

HeyMan, munching on a corn dog, says, "I bet they have a butter-eating contest."

"I wouldn't eat *that* butter," Cyn says, reading the pamphlet.

"Too fattening?" I say.

"No. It says here that after the fair, they melt it down and freeze it, then use it next year to make another cow. That butter is *way* past its expiration date."

"A butter contest would be cool," I say as we move on. "Only with fresh butter."

"My sister's cat once ate a whole stick," HeyMan says. "She wasn't too happy afterward. Neither of them were."

"What next?" I ask Cyn. "Want to go see the giant pig?"

"I want to see the textile exhibit. The quilts and hooked rugs. You guys don't have to come. We can meet up at the pizza thing later." She checks her phone. "It's in one hour."

"I'll look at quilts with you," HeyMan says, surprising both of us.

"Seriously?" Cyn says.

"Sure, why not?" He eats the last bite of his corn dog and looks at me. "You up for quilts, dude?"

"I want to check out the Pizza Shack," I say. "Get a sense for how it's set up." Also, I don't feel like being an extra on *The Cyn and Hay Show.*

"Cool. We'll be there at noon to cheer you on." HeyMan steers Cyn toward a mini-donut stand.

WATER

Papa's Pizza Shack is on Walnut Square, between the Giant Slide and the horse-and-cattle barns. Screaming kids on one side, and the powerful smell of manure on the other. Probably not the best location for a food concession, but Papa's stand has been there for twenty years, and he sells a lot of slices. The Pizza Shack always has a line.

This year, it's bigger, like Vito said. They've tacked on an addition, doubling its size. The old Papa's Pizza Shack sign has been replaced by a twenty-foot-long neon sign featuring a new name:

Papa Pigorino's Pizza Emporium
Home of the World-Famous Pigorino Bowl

The sign is festooned with American and Italian flags. In front of the stand, about fifty feet away, right in the middle of Walnut Square, a forty-foot-long table decorated with red, white, and green bunting sits atop a four-foot-high stage. Two men are setting up folding chairs at the table.

But what is really impressive is the line, hundreds of people long, running from the pizzeria, past the stage, and snaking back and forth across the square. Everywhere I look, people are chowing down on big floppy slices of Pigorino's pizza. It's unbelievable. Papa's pizza is good, but it's not *that* good.

I recognize a girl I know from school—Emily Keller— standing in the middle of the line with a girl I don't know.

"Hey Emily, what's going on?"

"Hi David," Emily says. "I hear you're going to be in the contest."

"That's the plan."

"This is my friend Alicia Moreno," she says. "Alicia just moved to Vacaville."

Alicia is shorter than Emily, and she has long black hair pulled back in a ponytail. She smiles and examines me with her shiny dark eyes. "You're really going to be in the contest?"

"I'm going to win it," I say with more confidence than I feel.

< 229 >

"That is so cool!" She seems genuinely impressed. I'm not used to girls telling me I'm cool.

"Thanks." I feel awkward. Maybe she's shining me on. "Uh . . . what's with the big line?"

Emily shows me a coupon. "They were handing these out at the Grandstand."

****** State Fair Special ******
FREE PIZZA
11–12 P.M.
SATURDAY ONLY!
Papa Pigorino's Pizza Emporium
(formerly Papa's Pizza Shack)

"I guess Papa wants to make sure we get a good crowd," I say.

Alicia says, "We'll be cheering for you, David."

I see a flash of white linen over by the serving window. It's Papa himself, working the crowd. I make my way over to him.

"Hi Papa," I say.

"Dustin!"

"It's David."

"David! I know you-a David. The big eater from-a Vacaville! You win-a this thing for Papa, hokay?"

< 230 >

"That's the plan," I say. "You sure you're going to have enough pizzas?"

"We got-a lots-a pizza. You want-a free slice?"

"I'll save myself for the contest." I swallow. My throat is dry. "Maybe a cup of water?"

"Hokay, water I get you." He snaps his fingers and shouts at one of the pizza servers. A moment later she brings me a paper cup full of water. I drink it in one gulp.

"See?" Papa says. "I take-a care-a my favorite customer. Now you go see Vito and get signed in."

Vito is sitting at a small table behind the stage. I head over there. A few other guys are milling around the table. Vito is talking to each of them, crossing their names off a list, and giving out name badges. As I reach the table, Vito is arguing with a scruffy, potbellied man with long blond hair.

"I don't see you on the list," he says.

"Look harder," the scruffy man says. He is wearing a neon-yellow-and-orange Hawaiian shirt beneath a loose camouflage pocket vest. A pair of baggy green cargo shorts completes his ensemble. "I won the qualifier in Chicago."

Vito runs his finger down the list. "It says here the Chicago event was won by some guy named . . . uh . . . G-U-R—"

"Gurgitator. El Gurgitator. That's my *stage* name, man." He produces a business card. "See? That's me. But when you make the check out, you make it out to Virgil B. Schutlebecker."

"You have to win before any check gets made out to anybody," Vito says, plainly irritated.

"Don't you worry, guy. I got it in the bag."

I am standing a few feet away, paralyzed. *The Gurge.* My nemesis. What is *he* doing *here*? What was he doing eating pizza in Chicago when he was supposed to be at Coney Island eating hot dogs? Then I remember what Cyn told me, that the Gurge had been barred from the Nathan's Famous contest.

"So what name do you want on your name tag?" Vito asks.

"How about El Gurge," he says. "G-U-R-G-E."

Vito writes *EL GURGE* in black marker on a name tag.

"Thanks, guy," the Gurge says, snatching the name tag from Vito's hand. "You can make out my check anytime." He laughs, showing his big white teeth, and turns toward me. His close-set pale-blue eyes meet mine, then travel down to my pepperoni T-shirt. "Nice shirt, kid." He smirks and brushes past me.

El Gurge. My heart is pounding and I can hardly breathe. I have never hated anyone as intensely as I am hating the Gurge at this moment. I want to run after him and grab him by his greasy hair and pound his stupid

< 232 >

face into the ground, but I can't move. It's probably just as well—he outweighs me by a hundred pounds.

How am I going to beat the Gurge? For all his despicableness, he's one of the top pros on the planet. He holds world records in everything from apple pie to deep-fried zucchini. I feel as if all hope has been sucked out of me.

"Hey David," Vito says. "Glad you made it. You see that guy I was just talking to?"

I nod.

"I want you to get up there and kick his ass."

"Okay." I take my name tag.

"Your seat number is on the back. By the way, Papa's agreed to go with plain cheese pizzas this time—no BLDs. Thanks for the suggestion."

"You're welcome."

"I'll be rooting for you."

I nod dully and move off. My only hope now is to win second prize: free pizzas for a year. Or third prize, the pizza cutter, because Egon Belt will probably beat me too.

‹ 43 ›

SNOW CONE

I am sitting on the grass hugging my knees on the far side of the square when a shadow falls across me.

"Bring your appetite, son?" It's Egon Belt, looking crisp and clean in his overalls and John Deere cap.

I give him a sickly smile. "I have an appetite; only guess who I just met. El Gurgitator."

"Virgil?" Egon Belt shrugs. "Heard he might show up."

"You ever beat him?"

"Nope. But I aim to give 'er a go. We got a shot, son."

"You really think so?"

"Yep, I do. I knew Virgil when he was a scrawny little kid like you. His mama had to drive him to his first contest. Nice lady. She lives in Galena, just the other side of Dubuque. Pretty town."

"Hard to imagine the Gurge having a mother."

"We all got a mama, son. Virgil's just a man with an appetite and an attitude. He can be beat."

"Yeah, but he's *fast*."

"Tortoise and the hare, son. Ten minutes is a long time. Virgil's got jaws, but he's got no heart. That boy is gonna crash and burn one day. Maybe this is the day. Keep an eye on him, though. He's got some tricks up his sleeve, and they ain't all kosher."

Papa's bullhorn-amplified voice booms across the square. "CONTESTANTS! ALL-A PIGORINO BOWL CON-TESTANTS TAKE-A THEIR SEATS!"

"That's our call. Good luck, son." Egon Belt turns and walks across the square toward the stage.

I stand. My legs feel rubbery, and I'm not in the least bit hungry, even though I haven't eaten a thing since last night. As I start toward the stage, Cyn and HeyMan find me. HeyMan is slurping a blueberry snow cone.

"Dude, hurry up! It's gonna start any second."

Several of the contestants are already on the stage.

"Are you okay?" Cyn asks.

"No. Guess who's here."

They wait for me to tell them.

"El Gurgitator," I say.

"The Gurge?" HeyMan says.

"He won the Chicago qualifier. He's the second- or

third-fastest eater on the planet. He even beat Joey Chestnut at the chicken-neck contest."

"Yeah, but this is pizza. Pigorino's pizza—your specialty."

I shake my head. "I don't know."

I look at their concerned faces and feel even worse.

"I'm really sorry," I say.

Cyn gets in front of me and forces me to look her in the eyes. Her face is only inches from mine, and I think I've never seen her this way, so close.

"You can do this," she says, squeezing my hands. "I know you can." She releases me. I walk slowly up to the stage. I check the back of my ticket. Seat number thirteen. It figures. I climb the six steps and find my chair. I'm right in the middle. Two chairs to my right sits Egon Belt. He catches my eye and winks.

"Good luck, son," he says.

I nod. "You too."

Most of the seats are filled when the Gurge thumps into the chair between me and Egon Belt. Great. I have to sit right next to him.

The Gurge turns to Egon Belt and feigns surprise. "Egon Belt? Aren't you getting kind of old and decrepit for this?"

"Can it, Virgil," Egon Belt says. "I'm old enough not to be psyched out by the likes of you."

< 236 >

"Ha! Nobody's immune to the power of the Gurge! I'm betting you have a Reversal before you finish one pie." He elbows me. "Am I right, kid?"

I refuse to look at him.

"THREE MINUTES!" Papa bellows.

The crowd is gathering in front of the stage. There must be five hundred people out there. Pigorino's employees are bringing out the pizzas in boxes. They set two boxes in front of each of us, plus two tall plastic water glasses.

The Gurge is talking loudly to everybody and nobody. "Yeah, me and Joey Chestnut, we once went *mano a mano* at a Pizza Hut in Kansas. I put down eighty slices to his seventy. It was epic. We split a bucket of jalapeño poppers for dessert. Yeah, I got this one wrapped and bagged. You all oughta just go home right now."

If the Gurge's trash talk is supposed to make me and everybody else mad, it's working. I look down the table. A lot of big guys, and only one woman, also on the large side. It doesn't matter. I just have to do my best and hope to win a pizza cutter and not embarrass myself.

Papa is pacing back and forth in front of us, going through the rules. They're the same as before, so I only half listen. One of the contestants asks what happens if we finish the two pizzas in front of us.

"We got-a lot-a pizzas," Papa says. "Pizzas keep coming. We no run out."

I scan the crowd and pick out Cyn and HeyMan near the front. Standing next to them is Hoover.

"You go, little David!" Hoover yells.

A few yards to his left I see Emily and Alicia. Alicia smiles and waves.

"Two minutes!" Papa yells, forgetting to use his bullhorn.

"Tell you what," the Gurge says, standing up. "I'm gonna give you all a five-minute head start, just to make it fair."

"Virgil, I do not believe the word *fair* belongs in your vocabulary," Egon Belt says in a relaxed drawl.

"ALL CONTESTANTS MUST BE SEATED FOR CONTEST TO BEGIN!" Papa shouts into his bullhorn, aiming it straight at the Gurge from three feet away. Startled, the Gurge sits back down.

"That dude is loud," he mutters.

Egon Belt smiles.

"ONE MINUTE!" Papa announces.

The Gurge leans closer to me. "That BLD thing at the qualifier was the biggest pizza I ever saw. How many slices you eat?"

I don't answer him. He shrugs.

"The competition in Chicago was weak," he says. "I only had to eat two."

"Two slices?" I say.

< 238 >

"Two pies."

Two BLDs? That's more than double what Egon Belt and I were able to eat. I don't believe it, but at the same time there's a small part of me that wonders if it might be true.

"THIRTY SECONDS!"

I look at the Gurge, at those little blue eyes and the smirk on his fat cheeks, and suddenly I am sure. He's lying, just trying to psych me out.

"TEN!"

He's a total scumbag and a cheat and a thief, and I want nothing more than to destroy him.

"NINE!"

I think about that phony dried-up half hot dog and my mom's two thousand dollars, and my heart is going like a trip-hammer.

"EIGHT!"

The crowd is still getting bigger—the bullhorn is drawing in fairgoers like hogs to a dinner bell.

"SEVEN!"

I look at HeyMan and Cyn. He puts his arm around her.

"SIX!"

The Gurge's fingers are resting on top of his first pizza box. We're not supposed to touch the boxes until Papa says go, but I'm the only one who notices.

"FIVE!"

I take a deep breath and imagine my stomach as an infinite space, big enough to hold the whole world.

"FOUR!"

My jaws are made of titanium, powered by an atomic engine. My teeth are blades of diamond.

"THREE!"

Emily and her friend Alicia are pressed right up against the front of the stage. Alicia raises her hand and pumps her fist.

"TWO!"

I peek at the Gurge. His eyes are drilling into the box. I see beads of sweat gathering on his forehead. He licks his lips. It's not a hungry lick; it's a nervous lick. He isn't sure he'll win.

"ONE!"

Time to focus . . .

"GO!"

⟨ 44 ⟩

GO, DAVID, GO

The Gurge is an animal. He doesn't hesitate for an instant—his box is open and the first slice disappears down his gullet like a rabbit being chased into its hole. He's on his second slice before I take my first bite. I fold, bite, bite, bite, and dump the crust in my water while grabbing my second slice with my other hand. The Gurge is on number three.

Don't look at him, I tell myself. *Focus!* I push myself, putting down the second slice in record time, add the crust to the water glass, take out the first crust and slam it down. I'm hitting a rhythm, and my first pizza is down the hatch at just over the two-minute mark.

I open the second box and glance at the Gurge. He's

two slices ahead of me. Egon Belt is also into his second pizza. My hands and jaws are working so fast I can't believe they are ahead of me, but I keep going.

The crowd is yelling. Papa is shouting into his bullhorn but I can't understand a word of it except when he calls out the minutes. Another boxed pizza appears in front of me. A couple of the eaters have already given up—the serious action is at the middle of the table: the Gurge, Egon Belt, and me. But as fast as I eat, I can't quite catch up with either of them. The Gurge is tearing into his pizza like a starving hyena—bits of crust fly, and sauce dribbles down his scruffy chin. He's making snorting and hacking sounds, but the pizza keeps disappearing into him. Egon Belt is going at it hard, too, but still manages to look relaxed. He's the Zen master of eating.

We're almost done with pizza number three at the five-minute mark when I see something out of the corner of my eye. The Gurge is reaching with his left hand into the side pocket of his vest while shoving a slice into his mouth with his right hand. He comes out with something—his hand almost covers it, but I think it's a small plastic squeeze bottle. I keep eating. He quickly transfers the bottle to his right hand. Whatever he's doing, it's clear that he doesn't want anybody to notice.

For the next several seconds, the Gurge eats with only his left hand. It doesn't slow him down much, if at all. He keeps darting glances at Egon Belt. At one point Egon Belt turns his head to look to his right, and I see a thin jet of liquid arc up from under the edge of the table.

Whatever's in the bottle, some of it is now on Egon Belt's pizza.

The Gurge returns the bottle to his vest pocket and attacks his pizza with renewed vigor. The two of them are neck and neck, and I'm still trailing by two slices. I take it up a notch, pushing my body to the max. My throat opens, and I find I can swallow with less chewing. Soaking the crusts in water is working—I notice a couple of the other eaters have adopted my technique. The food is moving into my body like a huge oregano-flavored snake.

I'm starting pizza four when I have to stand and do the Joey Jump to pack down what's in my stomach. I look up and down the table. Three chairs to my left, a guy wearing a Minnesota Vikings jersey—he looks like he might actually *be* a Minnesota Viking—is coming from behind. He's only one or two slices behind me. To my right, I see Egon Belt has stopped eating. His face is red and slick with sweat. He tries to stand up, falls to his knees, turns his head away from the table, and erupts.

"Reversal!" The Gurge thrusts his greasy fists up in triumph, and the plastic bottle pops out of his pocket and falls to the stage. "We have a Reversal of Fortune!"

Egon Belt is crawling off the stage, retching horribly.

While the Gurge is distracted, I bend over and pick up the squeeze bottle.

The Gurge turns back to his pizza and continues to demolish it. I do the same. I'm in second place, and I want to stay there. After it's over, I can take the bottle to Papa and tell him what I witnessed. Maybe the Gurge will get disqualified. I keep on eating. The Gurge looks over at my quickly disappearing pizza. He drops his left hand beneath the edge of the table. A second later his rock-hard fist backhands me hard in the belly. I double over, gasping in pain. The contents of my stomach are oozing up into my esophagus.

The Gurge keeps eating as if nothing happened. I squeeze my eyes shut, tears of pain and rage coursing down my cheeks. *Keep it down!* It takes several breaths, but I manage to reverse the impending Reversal. I open my eyes. The Gurge is ahead by almost four slices, and the Vikings guy is ahead by one. I grab a fresh slice and slam it down.

"Three minutes!" Papa shouts into his bullhorn.

The Gurge is inhaling slices at a staggering rate. He thinks he has the contest won—I can see it in his face. My stomach is still throbbing from his underhanded punch. Something clicks inside me. Without giving myself time to think about it, I point toward the far end of the table and say to him, "Gurge! Over there! Check it out."

< 244 >

When he turns his head to look, I empty the entire contents of the squeeze bottle onto his pizza.

"What?" he says, looking back at me.

"Never mind." I keep eating, and soon regain my rhythm. I'm starting on pizza number five when I hear a choking sound coming from the Gurge. He stands up and staggers back from the table. I don't bother to look back as I hear the sound of forty slices of masticated pizza reversing course.

The Gurge has regurgitated.

The Vikings fan has pulled ahead. Several of his friends are pressed up against the front of the stage, shouting, "Go, Turk! Go, Turk! Go, Turk!"

The only thing that can save me now is a miracle. He's too fast, too big, too bottomless—and I'm running out of room.

"Go, Turk! Go, Turk!"

I'm on the edge of despair when another voice reaches my ears.

"David! Go!"

I know that voice. I look up.

"David! Go!"

I see him now, sitting up high, way in back, on somebody's shoulders. The sunlight glints off his headphones and sunglasses. It's Mal.

"Go!" he shrieks, his high-pitched voice cutting through the noise. "Go!"

It's Dad holding him up. Mom is there, too.

I go. I go like the Gurge on steroids.

"David! Go!"

I go. I go like Takeru Kobayashi. I go like Joey Chestnut. I go like Jooky Garafalo.

"Go!"

I shove slices of pizza in my mouth, and they are transported magically to my stomach. At the nine-minute mark, I'm into my sixth pizza. I don't even bother to look at the Vikings guy.

"David! Go!"

I keep going. As long as Mal keeps yelling my name, I'm not about to stop.

< 246 >

⟨ 45 ⟩
FIFTY SLICES

I don't even know I've won at first, even though *everybody* is yelling my name.

"David! David! David!"

Papa grabs my wrist and pulls me to my feet and raises my hand high.

"David! David!"

I look over at the Vikings guy. He's staring at me in shock.

A high, thin voice cuts through the rest.

"David!"

I see Mal, still on Dad's shoulders, at the back of the crowd.

"Okay!" I try to shout, but what comes out is a croak.

Things get kind of confusing after that. People are climbing up onstage and shoving cameras and phones in my face and asking me questions. One of them says she's a reporter from the *Des Moines Register*.

"What's it like to eat fifty slices of pizza?" she asks.

Fifty? I ate *fifty* slices of pizza?

"Okay," I say. One word is all I can manage.

"You don't seem too happy about it," she says with a frown.

I shrug. I don't know if I'm happy or not—I'm mostly incredibly full, and I want to lie down. After a few minutes, Papa and Vito manage to clear the stage, so it's just me and the Vikings guy. The third-place winner has tottered off in a daze, not bothering to collect his Papa Pigorino Signature Pizza Cutter.

Papa presents me with a check for five thousand dollars, and that sets off another round of photos. He puts his arm around me and makes a short speech about how great Pigorino's pizzas are. He finally releases me and presents the second-prize gift certificate to the Vikings guy, who looks as if he never wants to see another Pigorino's pizza for the rest of his life. I know how he feels.

I climb off the back of the stage, wishing somebody would roll me up in a rug. I stagger off, looking for HeyMan and Cyn, or my parents, but before I find them I come across the Gurge. He is sitting on the ground with his back to a trash container looking dismally pale and miserable. He fixes his beady blue eyes on me.

< 248 >

"You," he says.

I pull the empty squeeze bottle from my pocket and toss it in his lap. "You droppod this."

He stares bleakly down at the bottle, takes a shuddering breath, and closes his eyes. I leave him to his misery.

I ride home with Mom, Dad, and Mal. Dad is driving. I have the front passenger seat tipped back, because with fifty slices of pizza in me I don't fold so good. Mom and Mal are in back. Nobody talks much at first. I know they're mad at me, even if at the same time they're a little bit proud of me for winning. We're out of Des Moines and on the highway when Dad clears his throat.

"David, you're right."

Nothing he could have said would have surprised me more.

"About what?"

"I'm going to tell you a secret," he says. "We don't know what we're doing."

"We who?"

"Your mother and I. There is no college degree in parenting. You have kids, and all of a sudden you have to make a million impossible choices. You make mistakes. You try to be fair, and you fail. Your sister, you know how smart she is, how good she is in school, and we're proud of her for that."

"Really? I never noticed." I can't keep the sarcasm out of my voice.

"You also know that Bridgette sometimes tries a little too hard. She can be needy, always begging for praise. She's been like that since she was a toddler, and I suppose we encouraged it. She craves approval and support—she demands it—and we give it to her, occasionally to excess."

I look back at Mom. She nods, and I realize that what Dad is saying, whatever he's getting at, is coming from both of them.

"And Mal is . . . Mal."

"Go," Mal says.

"Which leaves you stuck in the middle. You're the easy one, David. You've never demanded much from us, and you always seem to do okay—despite the poor judgment you showed using your mother's credit card. You're a low-maintenance kid."

"Great," I say. "I'm a Toyota."

"That is not a bad thing. Would you rather be a bundle of insecurities like your sister? Or developmentally disabled like Mal?"

"Okay," Mal says.

"Anyway, what I—your mom and I—want to say is this. We're not perfect, and we know you don't get acknowledged for everything you do, but we love you and we're proud of you and we're grateful for you every single day."

I stare at my knees. My eyes are stinging a little, but I manage not to cry.

"The other thing we want to say is that you're not off the hook. Your actions—stealing from your mother and participating in that contest against our wishes—tell us that you have to prove to us you can be trusted. You're going to have to work at it. And so long as you are living under our roof, there will be no more eating contests."

The way I'm feeling right now, that's fine by me.

< 251 >

IPECAC

According to Cyn, the stuff in the squeeze bottle was most likely syrup of ipecac.

Back in the twentieth century, you could buy ipecac in any drugstore. It was used as an emetic—something that makes you throw up. They used to give it to people who accidentally ate something poisonous.

"There are better treatments now," Cyn says, "and they don't sell it in drugstores anymore. The Gurge probably bought it online."

"Well, it sure works!"

It's the Monday after the Pigorino Bowl. Cyn and I are sitting on the patio watching Mal unscrew the big bolt holding together the legs of the picnic table. He's wearing his sunglasses but not his headphones. Dad is at work, and Mom is helping out at the church rummage sale.

"What are you going to do?" Cyn asks.

"Obviously I can't go to Papa. If I tell him I'm the one who spiked the Gurge's pizza, he might disqualify me and take the money back. Anyway, I don't think he wants his Pigorino Bowl to be ruined by scandal. But I feel bad for Egon Belt. If the Gurge hadn't cheated, Egon might have won."

"Or the Gurge might've won," Cyn says. "Makes you wonder why he did it, since he was already ahead."

"He's the Gurge," I say. "Hey Mal!"

Mal looks at me through his sunglasses.

"Be careful with that. You pull the bolt all the way out, the table might fall down."

"Okay David Go," Mal says. He continues to fiddle with the bolt.

"Mal has become quite the conversationalist," Cyn says.

"Yeah, he has four words now."

"Four? What's the fourth?"

"Kohlrabi."

"Kohlrabi? Like that vegetable that nobody eats?"

"Yeah. He started saying it on the way home from the fair. Mom says she's going to try to get him to eat some. I'll be surprised if he goes for it. He thinks it means potato chips."

"How are things with you and your mom?" Cyn asks.

"As good as can be expected, seeing as I stole two grand from her."

"At least they showed up to cheer for you."

"I think my dad was originally planning to come and yank me off the stage and drag me home. But then Mal flipped out when Dad tried to leave the house without him. He started screaming 'Go, David, Go!' over and over. Mom couldn't believe he all of a sudden had two new words. It was her idea to bring him to the fair. She thinks he's on the verge of becoming the next Shakespeare, once he learns to write. Mal's pretty good at getting what he wants."

"Hay asked me to ask you when your loyal investors get paid."

"I signed the check over to my mom. She'll deposit it in her account, and I'll have her write you guys your checks."

"Your mom's keeping the rest of the money?"

"We're negotiating. She thinks it should go to my college fund. She wants to have a *talk* when she gets home. I'm not looking forward to it."

"Maybe this will help. I found—"

She is interrupted by a crash. The picnic table has collapsed on one side, forming a little lean-to. Mal is tucked underneath it, looking out at us.

"Mal made himself a house," Cyn says.

"Are you okay, buddy?" I ask.

"Okay," he says, smiling happily.

"Good job, Mal." I turn to Cyn. "You were saying you found something?"

"I found Jooky Garafalo."

As much as I want to hear about Jooky, my first priority is to get Mal out from under the table before it collapses completely. I coax him out by promising him kohlrabi. We go inside, and I find him the bag of potato chips Mom hid in the cupboard.

When I get back outside, Cyn says, "Jooky works at Vock's Vinyl, a used-record store in Newark, New Jersey."

"Can you hold the table up for a sec?"

Cyn grabs the side of the table and lifts so I can slide the bolt back in. I screw the nut back on the bolt as tight as I can with my fingers.

"How did you find him?" I ask.

"Internet magic," Cyn says.

I crawl out from under the table and give it a shake. It feels solid enough.

"Seriously," I say, sitting down on the bench seat.

"Well, it took a while." Cyn sits next to me. "I started by looking for Garafalos. It turns out that there are more Garafalos in New Jersey than anywhere. You know how Jooky has all those fast-food-logo tattoos? I checked out all the tattoo parlors in New Jersey. Most of them have web-sites with pictures of their work. One shop called Payne and Gaines specializes in corporate-logo tats. They had a shot of one of Jooky's arms on their site."

"You are amazing," I say.

"I know! So I called them and told one of the owners, Mickey Payne, that I wanted to get in touch with one of his customers. I described Jooky's tattoos, and he said, 'Oh, that's Jeremy Garafalo, only he calls himself Jooky now.' He said he didn't know where Jooky lived, but he told me where he works."

"He just told you?"

"Not at first, but I said I was a reporter for BuzzFeed and we were doing an article on the ten best tattoo parlors in the U.S. He got all excited and told me all kinds of stuff." She takes out her phone and her thumbs become a blur. "I just texted you everything, including the phone number of the record store. Did you know that Jooky has a Burger King tattoo on his left butt cheek?"

"Um . . . why would I know that?"

"You wouldn't, and that's the point. Mickey Payne said Burger King wouldn't give Jooky any sponsorship money, so he put their logo on his butt."

"Have I told you how amazing you are?"

She smiles at me. "Not in the last twenty seconds."

"Hay thinks you're amazing, too."

She looks away. "Yeah, we've been hanging out a lot lately."

"I noticed."

She shrugs and gives me a sideways look. "Hay's more mature these days."

"So, are you guys . . ."

"I don't know." She tosses her hair in a girlie gesture that is not like Cyn at all.

"I do. You're in love with him."

"I'm more in *like* with him. I like you, too, but in a different way."

"I get it." I *do* get it, and the funny thing is, I think it's cool. I'm happy for them. For a while I thought maybe I was jealous, but I'm not. Just a little envious. I'm wondering how it will be for the three of us, how it will change. "We're still going to do things together, right? You guys aren't going to get all weird?"

"We've always been weird." Cyn grabs my hand and squeezes. "All for one, and one for all."

"The Three Musketeers?"

Cyn smiles and nods.

< 257 >

‹ 47 ›

CHICKEN SOUP

After Cyn leaves, I pick up my phone and retrieve her text with the record-shop number. I'm shaking so hard, I keep hitting the wrong keys, but finally I get a connection.

"Vock's Vinyl." The guy who answers the phone sounds like a gravel truck.

"Is Jooky there?"

I hear the guy rumble, "Yo, Jook."

A few seconds later, Jooky Garafalo himself is on the line.

"Yah, man."

"Jooky? Jooky Garafalo?" My voice has gone all creaky.

"How many guys named Jooky you know? What can I do you for?"

"Uh, my name's David Miller. I'm calling from Iowa, and I'm your number-one fan."

"Oh yeah? Cool. Iowa. You got corn there, right? That corn-on-the-cob contest?"

"Uh, yeah. But I just called to say I think you're the best, and . . . I'm sorry about Nathan's this year. I was rooting for you."

"No biggie, bro. I just couldn't find my flow."

"I have a question. You know that half dog?"

"Dude, did you call me just to remind me of my worst days?"

"No! I'm calling about that Certificate of Authenticity you signed for the Gurge."

He doesn't say anything for a second; then, "Aw, man, tell me you're not the chump bought that thing off Virgil."

"I sort of did. Is it real? The half dog?"

"Well . . . yeah, it was a half hot dog I didn't eat. But that thing I signed doesn't actually say it was the *particular* half dog that Chestnut beat me by. Virgil told me it was just a joke. Paid me twenty bucks to sign it. I didn't know he was gonna put it up on BuyBuy."

"Would you be willing to swear to that?"

"What, in court? That's a negatory, bro. I don't groove with the system. Sorry, dude. You got Gurged, and I feel for ya, man, but I'm out. I got records to sell and a pierogi contest comin' up next week."

I hang up, feeling defeated. If Jooky won't testify that the half dog is fake, I've got nothing.

Mal and Arfie, having finished their potato chips, come back outside. Mal is still wearing his shades. He immediately goes to the picnic table and starts fussing with the bolts. Arfie moves off to a safe distance to watch.

"Mal, cut it out."

Mal slides out from under the table.

"If you hurt yourself, Mom will kill me," I say.

"Okay." He wanders out into the yard with Arfie at his heels.

I think about what I just said—*Mom will kill me*—and that gives me an idea. I grab my phone and call directory assistance. It takes a few minutes, but I finally get a human being on the line.

"What city, please?"

"Galena, Illinois."

"Last name?"

"Schutlebecker." I spell it out.

"First name?"

"Um . . . Mrs.?"

Fortunately, there is only one Schutlebecker listing in Galena, Illinois.

Mrs. Schutlebecker is delighted to talk to me about her son, Virgil.

"He's famous, you know," she says.

"I know," I say. "He's one of the fastest eaters in the world."

"Yes, but I can't take credit for that. Our dinners at home were always quite civilized."

"I'm sure they were. Have you seen Virgil lately?"

"I'll be seeing him tonight. He's coming over for dinner, all the way from Rockford. Poor boy, he's been under the weather the past few days, so I'm making him my famous chicken soup."

"Did Virgil tell you about the hot dog he sold on BuyBuy?"

"No, I don't believe he did."

I tell her about the half dog—how Jooky Garafalo lost to Joey Chestnut, and how I found the half dog for sale on BuyBuy. Every so often she says, "Oh, my!" or "Oh, dear!" At one point, as I'm explaining how I think the AutoBuyBuy bidding was rigged—how the mystery bidder stopped as soon as I hit my limit—she interrupts me.

"I just don't see how that can be. Why, Darla works for them!"

"Darla?"

"Virgil's wife. She works for BuyBuy. They're based in Rockford, you know. I can't believe she would allow a mistake like that."

"Mrs. Schutlebecker, I don't think it was a mistake." I

take a deep breath. "I think your son and his wife rigged the system. The hot dog he sold me was a fake. I talked to Jooky Garafalo. He told me Virgil paid him twenty dollars to sign the fake certificate."

I'm not at all sure I've convinced her, or what she'll do even if she believes me, but I keep talking.

"I just thought you should know," I say after I'm done explaining. "Before I go to the police."

"Police? Why would you do that?"

"Your son stole two thousand dollars from me," I say.

She doesn't say anything, but I can hear the air whistling in and out through her nose.

"That boy," she says, a new, sharper tone entering her voice. "That boy will be the death of me. If I don't kill him first."

When Mom gets home, I'm under the picnic table using a wrench to snug up the leg bolts.

"What are you doing?" she asks.

"Fixing the table."

"It was broken?"

"Mal took it apart."

"Where is Mal?"

"In his room, rocking out."

"Oh. I bought some kohlrabi."

"I'm sure Mal will love it." *Not.*

Mal does not love kohlrabi.

The next morning, Mal and I are getting ready to go for a walk when the postal carrier delivers an Express Mail envelope postmarked Galena, Illinois. Inside is a check for two thousand dollars.

"Good news, Mal," I say.

"Okay, David." He puts on his headphones.

"Let's go show Mom."

Mom is at her desk working on her laptop. I hand her the check.

"See? I told you!"

She frowns and reads, "Katherine Schutlebecker . . . that would be this Virgil Schutlebecker's mother?"

"I guess so."

"I can see how Virgil turned into such a reprobate," she says. "Letting his mother pay for his misdeeds."

"He's still in trouble with *her*," I say. "No more chicken soup for him. In fact, Mrs. Schutlebecker told me she was going to dump the whole pot over his head when he showed up. I wonder if she did it."

"I wouldn't waste the soup," Mom says. "But I suppose every mother has her own way of dealing with her problem child." She narrows her eyes at me.

I give her my best grin. She tries to hold on to the stern

look, but her scowl breaks into a smile. She reaches up and rumples my hair.

"You're okay," she says.

"Okay!" Mal, sunglassed and headphoned, is using his outdoor voice.

"Hang on, Mal, we'll go in a minute." I look back at Mom. "Does this mean I get to keep the money I won?" I ask.

"For college," she says.

"Okay, but . . . *technically*, it's my money, right?"

"Technically?" she says. "*Technically*, you are a minor. *Technically*, you stole my credit-card number."

"I have to pay Cyn and HeyMan."

"I will write them checks, as I told you. But the other four thousand goes in your college fund."

"I was thinking about giving half of it to Egon Belt."

"Who is Egon Belt?"

"He's the reason I won."

"You want to give two thousand dollars to a man you hardly know?" Mom says.

"He let me tie him in the qualifier. He could have beat me, but he didn't. And if he hadn't got sick, he probably would have beat me Saturday."

"Yes, but if the situation were reversed, do you think he'd give *you* half his prize money?"

< 264 >

"I don't know. Does that matter? It's not about what somebody else would do; it's about what's right. Right?"

"It's a lot of money," she says.

"Suppose it was only ten bucks. What would be the right thing to do then?"

She doesn't have an answer for that.

"Wait a week," she says. "Think about it, okay?" She looks past me. "Your brother is waiting for you."

"Okay!" Mal shouts.

‹ 48 ›
HALIBUT

One week later, HeyMan and I ride our bikes ten miles to Halibut, Iowa.

"You sure you want to do this?" HeyMan says as we pedal up a long, shallow rise.

"How many times you going to ask me that?"

"How many times have I asked you so far?"

"At least five times in the last ten minutes."

"I'm gonna ask you all the way to Halibut."

"Give me a break, Hay. I've already been through this with my mom. She thinks I'm nuts, too."

"Your mother is a wise woman."

"Yeah, but she doesn't have to be *me*."

"What does that mean?"

"I mean I have to live with myself. If I don't do this, I'll feel guilty for the rest of my life."

"You'll get over it."

I decide to change the subject. "So what's the deal with you and Cyn?"

That takes him by surprise. He slows down as we reach the top of the hill.

"What do you mean?"

"Are you guys, you know, boyfriend-girlfriend?"

"I don't know," he says.

"How can you not know something like that?"

"Cyn says she wants to keep her options open."

"What options? We live in Vacaville!"

HeyMan speeds up. I pedal harder to catch him, and when I do, he says, "I guess you could say we're dating. But we're not exactly advertising it." We're riding side by side, but he doesn't look at me. "Are you cool with that?"

"Why wouldn't I be?"

"I don't know. Because we're the Three Musketeers?"

"Cyn and I talked about it, Hay. We're cool."

HeyMan nods. I can feel him relax.

"I think you guys would make a great couple," I say. We pedal the rest of the way to Halibut without talking.

Halibut is even smaller than Vacaville. HeyMan waits outside while I go into the town's only café—just a counter and half a dozen tables. The daily special is the loose-meat sandwich combo. From the looks of the sign, it's the daily special every day. I ask the waitress if she knows where Egon Belt lives.

"Egon?" she says. "Egon has a place over on the south end of town. Look for the house with everything perfect."

"What do you mean, 'everything perfect'?"

"You'll know it when you see it."

"Do you have an address?"

She laughs. "Child, this is Halibut. You go more than eight blocks in any direction, you'll either be wading through hog waste or lost in a cornfield." She points. "Just head down that way; you'll find Egon."

I go back outside.

"She says go south," I tell HeyMan.

"How far?"

"I don't know."

Four blocks away we come to a house that is, as the waitress said, perfect: a small one-story rambler painted blindingly white, with a matching white picket fence. Crisp black shutters frame the windows. The lawn is flat, utterly dandelion-free, and intensely green. The bushes in front are sculpted into precise cylinders. My dad would love it.

"It looks like a cartoon house," HeyMan says.

On the mailbox the name BELT is spelled out in perfect, perfectly spaced block letters.

"You want me to come with?" HeyMan asks.

"That's okay," I say. "I'll just be a minute."

I let myself in through the gate and walk up the short sidewalk. The pavers have been set in place with utmost precision. The doormat—WELCOME—is perfectly aligned with the edges of the landing. I press the doorbell. A few seconds later, the door opens.

Egon Belt is dressed exactly the same as always: neatly pressed coveralls that look brand-new, a crisp chambray shirt, and the full, perfectly shaped, uniformly gray beard. He doesn't say anything; he just looks at me.

"Hi," I say. "Remember me?"

"Certainly," he says. "Congratulations again."

"I wanted to give you this." I thrust the check at him.

He examines it without making a move to take it, then says, "Why?"

"Because the Gurge poisoned you. He squirted some stuff on your pizza."

"I know that," he says.

"You knew?"

He nods. "Virgil has used that nasty ipecac trick before. I blame myself—I wasn't paying attention."

"I saw it. I could have said something, but I didn't."

"Heat of the moment, son. It's not your responsibility to take care of the other contestants." He shrugs, then smiles. "It was almost worth it to see what happened next. That was a good move, giving Virgil a taste of his own medicine."

"You saw?"

"You weren't that smooth. You're lucky nobody else noticed."

"So you *knew* I cheated?"

Egon Belt laughs. "You didn't cheat, son. You took advantage of a situation, turned the tables, and eliminated the real cheater."

"But I should have said something. You should have won."

He shakes his head. "I wasn't about to catch up with Virgil. That boy was on fire. But he had that ipecac in his pocket, and he just couldn't stand not to use it."

"If he hadn't used it, you would have got second place at least."

"Free pizza for a year? No thank you. Anyway, I don't get up to Vacaville all that often."

"But I want to split my winnings with you."

"You're an idealist, son. I admire that in a young man. But I'm not going to take your money. I saw the way you put down those last two pizzas. The great Kobayashi himself would have bowed down to you. Fact is, if Virgil hadn't pulled his little stunt, I think you might've passed up the both of us. How many slices did you eat?"

"Fifty."

"Fifty." He shakes his head slowly. "Fifty! You keep that money, son. You earned it." He starts to close the door.

"Wait!"

"Yes?"

"Thank you. Thanks for letting me tie you at the qualifier."

"It was a legitimate tie. You have to learn to give yourself credit, son. Pat yourself on the back. It doesn't hurt. And spend that money on something besides pizza."

He closes the door. I look at the check, fold it, and put it back in my pocket.

"Well?" HeyMan says when I get back to the sidewalk.

"He told me to give myself a pat on the back and keep the money."

"That's what *I* told you. Except for the pat-on-the-back part."

"He said I might have won anyway."

"Do you think you would've?"

"I don't know. Maybe." I twist around.

"What are you doing?"

"Trying to give myself a pat on the back."

HeyMan reaches over and claps me on the shoulder. "There you go."

"Thanks. You hungry?"

"I could eat. You?"

"I could go for a loose-meat combo." I smile. "My treat."

< 272 >

< 49 >
MAL'S JOB

School started last week. I see HeyMan and Cyn every day, but we don't hang out as much as we used to. The boyfriend-girlfriend thing seems to be working for them. I have a girlfriend now too, sort of. Actually, I'm not sure what we are, but I've been seeing a lot of Alicia Moreno lately. She likes pizza almost as much as I do, but not the pizza they serve at school, so the two of us usually skip lunch and walk over to Pigorino's after school and split a sausage-and-mushroom. Two slices for her, the rest for me. At the moment we are more like eating partners than boyfriend-girlfriend, but you never know.

Bridgette has a new boyfriend, a guy named Gaarth, with two *a*'s. Gaarth has blond dreadlocks down to his shoulder blades, multiple studs in both ears, a ring in his right nostril, and he wears a serape. He starts every sentence with the word "Basically," as in, "Basically, the military-Industrial patriarchy is our species' suicide mechanism." Gaarth wants to study salamanders because, "Basically, when the amphibians go, we all go." He announced the first time we met him that he did not believe in having children. "Basically, we'll all be dead in fifty years, so what's the point in reproducing?"

I haven't seen any signs that Gaarth has a sense of humor, but he's a lot more interesting than Derek. Also, Mal likes him.

Mom and Dad were alarmed when Bridgette showed up wearing a nose ring of her own, but they seem to be coming around.

"Maybe it's just a phase," Mom says. "That's what college is for—to experiment, to try new things."

I don't know if she's talking about Gaarth or the nose ring. Probably both.

"I'm thinking about getting a tongue stud," I say.

Mom gives me the stink eye.

"Just kidding."

"You had better be. In any case, I'm sure one day Bridgette will meet her perfect young man."

"You mean perfect like I was?" Dad says.

"Even more perfect."

I've seen pictures of Dad in college. He looked kind of like Gaarth, only in a Nirvana T-shirt instead of a serape.

I'll be in college too before long, probably at a state school, because unlike Bridgette, my grades aren't exactly scholarship material. But I'm pretty sure I'll do okay, because I always figure things out—one way or another. I might enter some eating contests to help pay for it.

Mal will still be at home, of course. He will always be at home, despite Mom's dreams for him. Since the contest, he has learned two more words: "mine" and "Arfie." I think Mom's bummed that he still hasn't learned "Mom" or "Dad," but I know he'll get there. He has his own way of coming at things. I also know now that although I'm the middle kid in a typically messed-up family, I am not the slider that welds the two halves of the bun. That's Mal's job. I know that the way I know the sun will rise. But I also know he'll be okay, because we will always be here to take care of him, and Mal will be here for us, teaching us his Rules, holding us together.

ACKNOWLEDGMENTS

Writing may be an expression of one's inner self, but it is not a solitary act. None of us are truly alone, and for that we should be grateful.

With that in mind, I'd like to offer many thanks, beginning with my parents, who raised seven wild animals and gently nudged them to become human. And to my six amazing siblings, who inspire me every single day in countless ways.

To my Minnesota kid-lit friends, who form a vast and supportive community of writers, educators, and booksellers here in the Twin Cities, for the reality checks, the encouragement, the companionship, and the laughs.

To the team at Candlewick, whose love and passion for children's literature are unsurpassed, and especially to my editor, the redoubtable Katie Cunningham, who guided me to the heart of this book over a platter of sliders at Manny's.

To Nancy and Steve St. Clair, for their insights into six-hundred-pound butter cows and other Iowa arcana.

To my literary agent, Jennifer Flannery, who has stuck with me through two decades of genre-hopping madness.

Finally, and foremost, to my partner and muse, Mary Logue.

I thank you all.

DISCUSSION QUESTIONS

1. "Being the middle kid of three is like being the beef in a SooperSlider—you're just there to weld the bun together" (page 18). Why does David have such a low opinion of himself at the beginning of the novel? How does this change?

2. Mal has a Wall of Things in his room. What do you think these objects mean to him? What does David learn about his brother from the Wall?

3. Why doesn't the family call Mal autistic? What are the advantages and disadvantages of using that label? Are there labels you embrace or avoid?

4. "For every problem there is a solution" is a favorite saying of David's father (page 39). Is Mr. Miller too optimistic? Are there some problems that can't be solved?

5. David feels terrible thinking "Sometimes Mal feels like a huge ball and chain. Sometimes I wish he didn't exist" (page 68). How does each of the Miller family members cope with Mal?

6. What do you think is the significance of this book's title?

What *happened* in the woods that day?

PETE HAUTMAN

OTHER WOOD

Before he died, Grandpa Zach used to talk about weird stuff like quantum physics, secrets, lies, and haunted golf courses. Stuey didn't understand what he meant . . . until now.

★ "Will set imaginations spinning with possibilities."
—*Publishers Weekly* (starred review)

★ "Spellbinding." —*Kirkus Reviews* (starred review)

Available in hardcover and audio and as an e-book

www.candlewick.com